Penguin Books

Penguin Modern Stories 6

Edited by Judith Burnley

Penguin Books

Penguin Books Ltd, Harmondsworth,
Middlesex, England
Penguin Books Australia Ltd, Ringwood,
Victoria, Australia

First published in book form in Great Britain by
Penguin Books Ltd 1970

Made and printed in Great Britain by
Cox & Wyman Ltd,
London, Reading and Fakenham
Set in Intertype Baskerville

Contents

All these stories are published here for the first time in this country.

Elizabeth Taylor

Sisters

On a Thursday morning, soon after Mrs Mason returned from shopping – in fact she had not yet taken off her hat – a neat young man wearing a dark suit and spectacles, half-gold, half-mock tortoiseshell, and carrying a rolled umbrella, called at the house, and brought her to the edge of ruin. He gave a name, which meant nothing to her, and she invited him in, thinking he was about insurance, or someone from her solicitor. He stood in the sitting-room, looking keenly about him, until she asked him to sit down and tell her his business.

'Your sister,' he began. 'Your sister Marian,' and Mrs Mason's hand flew up to her cheek. She gazed at him in alarmed astonishment, then closed her eyes.

In this town, where she had lived all her married life, Mrs Mason was respected, even mildly loved. No one had a word to say against her, so it followed there were no strong feelings either way. She seemed to have been made for widowhood, and had her own little set, for bridge and coffee mornings, and her committee-meetings for the better known charities – such as the National Society for the Prevention of Cruelty to Children, and the Royal Society for the Prevention of Cruelty to Animals.

Her husband had been a successful dentist, and when he died she moved from the house where he had had his practice, into a smaller one in a quiet road nearby. She had no money worries, no worries of any kind. Childless and serene, she lived from day to day. They were almost able to set their clocks by her, her neighbours said, seeing her leaving the house in the mornings, for shopping and coffee at the Oak Beams Tea Room, pushing a basket on wheels, stalking rather on high-heeled shoes, blue-rinsed, rouged. Her front went down in a straight line from her heavy bust, giving her a stately look, the weight throwing her back a little. She took all of life at the same pace – a sign of ageing. She had settled to it a long time ago, and all of her years seemed the same now, although days had slightly varying patterns. Hers was mostly a day-time life, for it was chiefly a woman's world she had her place in. After tea, her friends' husbands came home, and then Mrs Mason pottered in her garden, played patience in the winter or read historical romances from the library. 'Something light,' she would tell the assistant, as if seeking suggestions from a waiter. She could never remember the names of authors or their works, and it was quite a little disappointment when she discovered that she had read a novel before. She had few other disappointments – nothing much more than an unexpected shower of rain, or a tough cutlet, or the girl at the hairdresser's getting her rinse wrong.

Mrs Mason had always done, and still did, everything expected of women in her position – which was a phrase she often used. She baked beautiful Victoria sponges for Bring and Buy Sales, arranged flowers, made *gros-point* covers for her chairs, gave tea-parties, even sometimes, daringly, sherry-parties with one or two husbands there, much against their will – but this was kept from her. She was occasionally included in other women's evening gatherings, for she made no difference when there was a crowd, and it was an easy kindness. She mingled, and chatted about other people's holidays and families and jobs. She never drank more than two glasses of sherry, and was a good guest, always exclaiming appreciatively at the sight of a plate of canapes, 'My goodness, *someone's* been busy!'

Easefully, the time had gone by.

This Thursday morning, the young man, having mentioned her sister, and seen her distress, glanced at one of the needlework cushions, and rose for a moment to examine it. Having ascertained that it was her work (a brief, distracted nod), he praised it, and sat down again. Then, thinking the pause long enough, he said, 'I am writing a book about your sister, and I did so hope for some help from you.'

'How did you know?' she managed to ask with her numbed lips. 'That she was, I mean.'

He smiled modestly. 'It was a matter of literary detection – my great hobby. My life's work, I might say.'

He had small, even teeth, she noticed, glancing at him quickly. They glinted, like his spectacles, the buttons on his jacket and the signet ring on his hand. He was a hideously glinty young man, she decided, looking away again.

'I have nothing to say of any interest.'

'But anything you say will interest us.'

'Us?'

'Her admirers. The reading public. Well, the world at large.' He shrugged.

'The world at large' was menacing, for it included this town where Mrs Mason lived. It included the Oak Beams Tea Room, and the Societies of Prevention.

'I have nothing to say.' She moved, as if she would rise.

'Come! You had your childhoods together. We know about those only from the stories. The beautiful stories. That wonderful house by the sea.'

He looked at a few shelves of books beside him, and seemed disappointed. They were her late husband's books about military history.

'It wasn't so wonderful,' she said, for she disliked all exaggeration. 'It was a quite ordinary, shabby house.'

'Yes?' he said softly, settling back in his chair and clasping his ladylike hands.

The shabby, ordinary house – the Rectory – had a path between cornfields to the sea. On either side of it now were caravan sites. Her husband, Gerald, had taken her back there once when they were on holiday in Cornwall. He, of course, had been in the know. She had been upset about the caravans, and he had comforted her. She wished that he were here this morning to deal with this terrifying young man.

Of her childhood, she remembered – as one does – mostly the still hot afternoons, the cornflowers and thistles and scarlet pimpernels, the scratchy grass against her bare legs as they went down to the beach. Less clearly, she recalled evenings with shadows growing longer, and far-off sounding voices calling across the garden. She could see the picture of the house with windows open, and towels and bathing-costumes drying on upstairs sills and canvas shoes, newly-whitened, drying, too, in readiness for the next day's tennis. It had all been so familiar and comforting; but her sister, Marian, had complained of dullness, had ungratefully chafed and rowed and rebelled – although using it all (twisting it) in later years to make a name for herself. It had never, never been as she had written of it. And she, Mrs Mason, the little Cassie of those books, had never been at all that kind of child. These more than forty years after, she still shied away from that description of her squatting and peeing into a rock-pool, in front of some little boys Marian had made up. 'Cassie! Cassie!' her sisters had cried, apparently, in consternation. But it was Marian herself who had done that, more like. There were a few stories she could have told about Marian, if she had been the one to expose them all to shame, she thought grimly. The rock-pool episode was nothing, really, compared with some of the other inventions – 'experiments with sex', as reviewers had described them at the time. It was as if her sister had been compelled to set her sick fancies against a background that she knew.

Watching Mrs Mason's face slowly flushing all over to

blend with her rouged cheekbones, the young man, leaning back easily, felt he had bided his time long enough. Something was obviously being stirred up. He said gently – so that his words seemed to come to her like her own thoughts – 'A few stories now please. Was it a happy childhood?'

'Yes. No. It was just an ordinary childhood.'

'With such a genius amongst you? How *awfully* interesting!'

'She was no different from any of the rest of us.' But she *had* been, and so unpleasantly, as it turned out.

'Really *extraordinarily* interesting.' He allowed himself to lean forward a little, then, wondering if the slightest show of eagerness might silence her, he glanced about the room again. There were only two photographs – one of a long-ago bride and bridegroom, the other of a pompous-looking man with some sort of chain of office hanging on his breast.

It was proving very hard-going, this visit; but all the more of a challenge for that.

Mrs Mason, in her silvery-grey wool dress, suddenly seemed to him to resemble an enormous salmon. She even had a salmon shape – thick from the shoulders down and tapering away to surprisingly tiny, out-turned feet. He imagined trying to land her. She was demanding all the skill and tenacity he had. This was very pleasurable. Having let him in, and sat him down, her good manners could find no way of getting rid of him. He was sure of that. Her good manners were the only encouraging thing, so far.

'You know, you are really not at all what I expected,' he said boldly, admiringly. 'Not in the very least like your sister, are you?'

What he had expected was an older version of the famous photograph in the Collected Edition – that waif-like creature with the fly-away fringe and great dark eyes.

Mrs Mason now carefully lifted off her hat, as if it were a coronet. Then she touched her hair, pushing it up a little. 'I was the pretty one,' she did not say; but, feeling some explanation was asked for, told him what all the world knew.

'My sister had poor health,' she said. 'Asthma and migraines, and so on. Lots of what we now call allergies. I never had more than a couple of days' illness in my life.' She remembered Marian always being fussed over – wheezing and puking and whining, or stamping her feet up and down in temper and frustration, causing scenes, a general rumpus at any given moment.

He longed to get inside her mind; for interesting things were going on there, he guessed. Patience, he thought, regarding her. She was wearing opaque grey stockings; to hide varicose veins, he thought. He knew everything about women, and mentally unclothed her. In a leisurely fashion – since he would not hurry anything – he stripped off her peach-coloured slip and matching knickers, tugged her out of her sturdy corselette, whose straps had bitten deep into her plump shoulders, leaving a permanent indentation. He did not even jib at the massive, mottled flesh beneath, creased, as it must be, from its rigid confinement, or the suspender imprints at the top of her tapering legs. Her navel would be full of talcum powder.

'It was all so long ago, I don't want to be reminded,' she said simply.

'Have you any photographs – holiday snapshots, for instance? I adore looking at old photographs.'

There was a boxful upstairs, faded sepia scenes of them all paddling – dresses tucked into bloomers – or picknicking, with sandwiches in hand, and feet out of focus. Her father, the Rector, had developed and printed the photographs himself, and they had not lasted well. 'I don't care to live in the past,' was all she said in reply.

'Were you and Marian close to one another?'

'We were sisters,' she said primly.

'And you kept in touch? I should think that you enjoyed basking in the reflected glory.' He knew that she had not kept in touch, and was sure by now that she had done no basking.

'She went to live in Paris, as no doubt you know.'

Thank heavens, Mrs Mason had always thought, that she *had* gone to live in Paris, and that she herself had married and been able to change her name. Still quite young, and before the war, Marian had died. It was during Mr Mason's year as Mayor. They had told no one.

'Did you ever meet Godwin? Or any of that set?'

'Of course not. My husband wouldn't have had them in the house.'

The young man nodded.

Oh, that dreadful clique. She was ashamed to have it mentioned to her by someone of the opposite sex, a complete stranger. She had been embarrassed to speak of it to her own husband, who had been so extraordinarily kind and forgiving about everything connected with Marian. But that raffish life in Paris in the thirties! Her sister living with the man Godwin or, turn and turn about with others of her set. They had all switched from one partner to the other; sometimes – she clasped her hands together so tightly that her rings hurt her fingers – to others of the same sex. She knew about it; the world knew; no doubt her friends knew, although it was not the sort of thing they would have discussed. Books had been written about that Paris lot, as Mrs Mason thought of them, and their correspondence published. Godwin, and Miranda Braun, the painter, and Grant Opie, the American, who wrote obscene books; and many of the others. They were all notorious: that was Mrs Mason's word for them.

'I think she killed my father,' she said in a low voice, almost as if she were talking to herself. 'He fell ill, and did not seem to want to go on living. He would never have her name mentioned, or any of her books in the house. She sent him a copy of the first one – she had left home by then, and was living in London. He read some of it, then took it out to the incinerator in the garden and burned it. I remember it now, his face was as white as a sheet.'

'But *you* have read the books surely?' he asked, playing her in gently.

She nodded, looking ashamed. 'Yes. Later, I did.' A terrified curiosity had proved too strong to resist: And, reading, she had discovered a childhood she could hardly recognize, although it was all there: all the pieces were there, but shifted round as in a kaleidoscope. Worse came after the first book, the stories of their girlhood and growing up and falling in love. She, the Cassie of the books, had become a well-known character, with all her secrets laid bare; though they were really the secrets of Marian herself and not those of the youngest sister. The candour had caused a stir in those far-off days. During all the years of public interest, Mrs Mason had kept her silence, and lately had been able to bask indeed – in the neglect which had fallen upon her sister, as it falls upon most great writers at some period after their death. It was done with and laid to rest, she had thought – until this morning.

'And you didn't think much of them, I infer,' the young man said.

She started, and looked confused. 'Of what?' she asked, drawing back, tightening his line.

'Your sister's stories.'

'They weren't true. We were well-brought up girls.'

'Your other sister died, too.'

He *had* been rooting about, she thought in dismay. 'She died before all the scandal,' Mrs Mason said grimly. 'She was spared.'

The telephone rang in the hall, and she murmured politely and got up. He heard her, in a different, chatty voice, making arrangements and kind inquiries, actually laughing. She rang off presently, and then stood for a moment steadying herself. She peered into a glass and touched her hair again. Full of strength and resolution, she went back to the sitting-room and just caught him clipping a pen back into the inside pocket of his jacket.

'I'm afraid I shall have to get on with some jobs now,' she said clearly, and remained standing.

He rose – had to – cursing the telephone for ringing, just

when he was bringing her in so beautifully. 'And you are sure you haven't even one little photograph to lend me,' he asked. 'I would take such enormous care of it.'

'Yes, I am quite sure.' She was like another woman now. She had been in touch with her own world, and had gained strength from it.

'Then may I come to see you again when you are not so busy?'

'Oh, no, I don't think so.' She put out an arm and held the door-handle. 'I really don't think there would be any point.'

He really felt himself that there would not be. Still looking greedily about him, he went out into the hall towards the front door. He had the idea of leaving his umbrella behind, so that he would have to return for it; but she firmly handed it to him. Even going down the path to the gate, he seemed to be glancing from side to side, as if memorizing the names of flowers.

'I said nothing. I said nothing,' Mrs Mason kept telling herself, on her way that afternoon to play bridge. 'I merely conveyed my disapproval.' But she had a flustered feeling that her husband would not have agreed that she had done only that. And she guessed that the young man would easily make something of nothing. 'She killed my father.' She had said that. It would be in print, with her name attached to it. He had been clever to ferret her out, the menacing young man, and now he had something new to offer to the world – herself. What else had she said, for heaven's sake? She was walking up hill, and panted a little. She could not for the life of her remember if she had said any more. But, ah yes! How her father had put that book into the incinerator. Just like Hitler, some people would think. And her name and Marian's would be linked together. Ex-mayoress, and that rackety and lustful set. Some of her friends would be openly cool, others too kind, all of them shocked. They would discuss the matter behind her back. There were even those who would say they were 'intrigued' and ask questions.

Mrs Oldfellow, Mrs Fitch and Miss Christy all thought she played badly that afternoon, especially Mrs Oldfellow who was her partner. She did not stay for sherry when the Bridge was over; but excused herself, saying that she felt a cold coming on. Mrs Fitch's offer to run her back in the car she refused, hoping that the fresh air might clear her head.

She walked home in her usual sedate way; but she could not rid herself of the horrible idea that they were talking about her already.

Elizabeth Taylor

The Excursion to the Source

'England was like this when I was a child,' Gwenda said. She was fifteen years older than Polly, and had had a brief, baby's glimpse of the gay twenties – though, as an infant, could hardly have been really conscious of its charms.

It was France – the middle of France – which so much resembled that unspoilt England. In the hedgerows grew all the wild flowers that urbanization, ribbon-development and sprayed insecticides had changed into delights of the past in the south of England where Gwenda and Polly lived.

Polly had insisted on Gwenda's stopping the car so that she could get out and add to her bunch some new blue flower she was puzzling over. She climbed the bank to get a good specimen and stung her bare legs on some nettles. Gwenda sat in the car with her eyes closed.

Polly, having spat into her palm and rubbed it on her smarting legs, began to search for the blue flower in *Fleurs de Prés et des Bois*, instead of looking at the map. Cross-roads were on them suddenly and she had no directions to give. Gwenda pulled to the side of the road, having taken the wrong turning, and reached for the map, screwing in her monocle. As she was studying the route, frowning, looking up at the sun for her bearings, Polly said, 'I suppose it's a sort of campanula. What on earth does *lancéolées* mean? Oh, I *wish* I'd brought my proper flower book from home.'

'It's *this* road we want,' Gwenda said, following it on the map with her nicotined finger. 'If you could remember, we turn off *here*, and about eight kilometres farther on bear right.' She handed back the map. Polly had scarcely glanced at it, but she took it obediently, although she could never read a map unless they were travelling north, which at present they were not.

'And when we've surmounted *that* little problem, you'd better look in the Michelin for somewhere for tonight,' Gwenda added, and began to wrench the car round grimly, as if it were a five-ton lorry.

It was ten years since she had been in this part of France; with her husband then. They had travelled along the Dordogne Valley, from the mouth to the source, crossing from bank to bank. It was in the year that he died, and she remembered with a turn of her heart, how, as she was driving, she would give secret glances at him, knowing him so well that he could never hide the signs of pain coming on – the difference in breathing, the slight shifting in his seat, the hand going involuntarily to his chest, and then at once returning to his lap to grip hold of the map. He could read maps whichever direction they were heading for.

Polly had put the flower book into the dashboard pocket and had her eyes on the Michelin guide. She was dreadfully short-sighted, but would not wear spectacles, however much Gwenda nagged her. She would not even use the subterfuge of lenses in sun-glasses, which had been suggested.

'There's one with two pairs of those scissors at a place called – I think it's Sebonac.'

'Selonac,' Gwenda said. 'How much?'

'I can't see.'

'I'll have a look later. Can you find it on the map?'

'I already have,' Polly said with pride.

Gwenda was always fussing about money – heading Polly off the Menu Gastronomique on to the eleven franc one. Although it was Polly's money, Polly sometimes thought.

Gwenda's husband had left her poorly provided for, and she had taken a job managing a hotel until Polly's mother, her own godmother, had begged her to look after Polly, *poor*

Polly she always called her, and administer her affairs. This was before the operation from which she did not recover (as the doctor put it). 'If anything should happen,' she had said. Polly was left very comfortably indeed. Long ago, people had thought Gwenda's parents clever to have chosen so rich a slight acquaintance to be Gwenda's godmother.

As soon as Mrs Hervey had died, Gwenda moved into her place; into the house in Surrey – red brick with a green dome, monkey-puzzle trees and dark banks of rhododendrons, everywhere smelling of pine trees. Polly was acquiescent. She could not have managed on her own. This was clear to everyone. And at twenty-seven it was thought unlikely that she would marry. In spite of the solid worth of her position, men seemed uncertain with her, found her scatter-brained and childish conversation maddening, wondered amongst themselves if she were really all there. She was like a lanky child with her pale, freckled face, soft, untidy hair, her awkwardness. She was forever tripping over carpets or walking into doors. She got on people's nerves.

The responsibility of having quite a little heiress on her hands was one Gwenda felt she could shoulder. She was ready to deal with impoverished widowers or ambitious younger men; but few came their way in Surrey. Fork luncheons for women was their manner of entertaining, or an evening's bridge which Polly did not join in. She would sit apart, sticking foreign stamps crookedly into an album. Besides stamps, she collected Victorian bun pennies, lustre jugs, fans, sea-shells, match-boxes and pressed wild flowers. There was a pile of albums full of pressed flowers, and what she seemed to love best about being in France was the chance of collecting different varieties. She hoped that Selonac, when they arrived there, would have more surprises. In a foreign country there was always the delight of not knowing what she might discover next – some rare strange orchid, perhaps, that she had never found before.

But Selonac was, at first sight, a disappointment – a few

straggling houses on either side of the road. They were nearly through it when they saw a sign – 'Auberge' – pointing down a lane to their right. 'There!' shouted Polly, trying to be efficient, but Gwenda was already turning the corner. They came to a little cobbled square, with a church and a baker's shop and a garage and the auberge – with one or two umbrellaed tables and some box trees in tubs on the pavement before it.

'I'll go and ask,' Gwenda said. She always did all the fixing-up, while Polly sat mooning in the car over her wild flowers, or squinting short-sightedly at the *Guide Michelin*, looking up for the twentieth time the difference between a black bath-tub and a white.

When Gwenda came back, she was followed by a young man, who dragged their suitcases out of the boot and lurched back into the darkness of the hotel with them.

It was a very dark hotel. It was silent, and smelled of ripe melon. Polly felt depressed, as she went upstairs after Gwenda. She was never asked for her opinions about where they should stay. They never shared a room, and Gwenda always told her which was hers – and it was never the one nearest the bathroom or with the best view. She was glad that sharing a room was not one of Gwenda's economies. Gwenda snored like a man. She had heard her through many a thin wall.

This time they both had the same view from their windows – across an orchard to a row of silvery trees which looked as if they bordered a stream. There was very little difference between the two rooms. Madame Peloux, the proprietress, showed them one after the other, as if there were any chance of Polly's making a choice; and then she began to chivvy her son, Jean, about the luggage. He was a clumsy, silent young man, and seemed to be sulking. His mother nagged him monotonously, as if from an old habit.

Like some wine, Polly did not travel well. She became more and more creased and greasy-faced. And the clothes in her suitcase, amongst the layers of tattered tissue-paper, all were creased, too, and all a little grubby, yet not *quite* grubby enough, she decided, to warrant all the fuss of getting them washed.

'Aren't you ready *yet*?' asked Gwenda at the door. 'After all that driving, what I need is some *violent* exercise.'

She usually said something like this, and once upon a time Polly had had amusing visions of her running across-country or playing a few chukkers of polo. Now she knew that all that would happen would be that Gwenda would drape her cardigan over her shoulders and go for a stroll round the garden, or amble round the village, stopping to look in shop-windows – longest at the charcuteries to marvel at the terrines. She examined them with a professional eye; for her own pâté was quite the talk of their part of Surrey. When she was asked for the recipe, she became carefully vague and said she had none; that she just threw in anything that came to hand.

This evening there was a pâté on the ten franc menu, so she was happy. She had had her stroll through the orchard, and Polly, still unpacking, had watched her from the bedroom window. Gwenda pushed her way through the long grass, lifting her neat ankles over briars. She had a top-heavy look, especially when viewed from above. Her large bosom was out of character, Polly thought. It was altogether too motherly-looking. And to think of Gwenda with children, was impossible.

In the end, the unpacking was done, and the little walk was over, and they went into the almost empty dining room. There were red and pink tablecloths, and large damp napkins to match, and Jean, Madame Peloux's son, had combed his frizzy hair, and was waiting inexpertly at table.

'Mosquitoes,' Gwenda was saying. 'I'm afraid there might be. I went up and closed the shutters.'

There *was* a stream at the bottom of the orchard, across a narrow lane. She had come to it on her wanderings, and had been bitten a little by midges.

'The pâté's not bad,' she said, dipping into the jar of gherkins.

Polly thought it a bit 'off' – well, sour anyway; but she said nothing. She was too often told that the taste she objected to, was the very one that had been aimed at, the absolute perfection of flavour.

Jean annoyed Gwenda by saying the name of everything he put on the table – as if she and Polly were children. 'Truites,' he announced, setting the dish down. They looked delicious – sprinkled with parsley and shredded almonds.

Gwenda, whose French – like everything else – was so much better than Polly's, asked if they were from the stream below the orchard, and Jean looked evasive, as if he could not understand her. 'Truities,' he said again and turned away, knocking over a glass as he did so.

The only other guests sat across the room. They were obviously not newcomers. They were favoured by the best table at the garden window, whereas Gwenda and Polly looked out on to the square. They had a bottle of wine with their room number scribbled on the label, and the man poured it out himself, looking very serious as he did so. The woman drank water, holding the glass in a shaking hand, tinkling it against her false teeth. She was ancient. He was in his sixties, and she was his mother.

As they were French, Gwenda had to listen with a little extra concentration to what they said – although they said little, and that in muted voices, as they stared before them, waiting for Jean to bring the next dish.

The old woman was thin and ashen and wore a sort of half-mourning of grey and mauve, and a hat – a floppy, linen garden hat. The only real colour about her was her crimson shiny lips, crookedly done, which she pressed and smudged, after every sip of water, with a purple handkerchief. Large diamond rings kept slipping on her old fingers.

'Mother and son,' Gwenda said in a low explanatory voice to Polly.

Jean had brought a large tart. Glazed slices of apple were slightly burnt. He made a great business of cutting it, frowning and pursing his lips as if it were a very tricky job.

Monsieur and Madame Devancourt, as he then addressed them, waved the tart away. Gwenda fastened on to the name; repeated it once or twice in her mind, and had it secure.

'How *good* not to have anything frozen,' she said, as she said at nearly every meal time.

'The tart is lovely,' Polly said. She loved sweet things, and longed for them through the other courses.

Madame Devancourt played with her rings and stared about her, while her tall, bald son was peeling an orange for her. They really were a very silent pair; but sometimes he made a little joke, and she gave a smothered snigger behind her handkerchief. It was surprising – sounded like a naughty little girl laughing in church.

Through the window, Polly watched one or two people sitting at the tables outside the inn, looking rather bored as they sipped their evening drink. A middle-aged woman, with a bitter, closed expression on her face, sat beside an older woman who was bowed-over, so hunch-backed that she kept losing balance and slipping sideways. Then the younger woman – she was obviously her daughter – would put her right, and turn her head away again, without a word. After a while, she suddenly stood up, got her mother to her feet and began a slow progress back across the square.

Jean brought coffee to Gwenda and Polly and slopped it into the saucers pouring it out. Gwenda asked for another saucer and when he brought it, he looked so sulky that Polly smiled up at him, and thanked him in her atrocious accent. She knew so well herself what it was like to be clumsy and inadequate.

'Such a moron,' Gwenda said. 'Never mind, it's only for one night.'

Although it turned out to be for six.

Gwenda always got up for breakfast. She found French beds uncomfortable, and 'liked to be about', as she put it.

The Devancourts were also up. Madame was wearing her floppy hat, and a pair of grubby tennis-shoes. Her son peeled another orange for her, and made a few more jokes. She seemed to be his life, and accepted his attentions placidly. But she was, in her own way, protective to *him*. When he half stood up, with his napkin in one hand and the orange in the other, and bowed to Gwenda and Polly as they came in, she stared hard at him, as if willing him back into his seat, and Polly could imagine her having guarded him from women since he was a young man; just as Gwenda had warded off young men from herself. When he had sat down again and resumed his careful orange-peeling, the old woman turned a cold and steady gaze on Gwenda, as if to say, 'Don't waste any time on *this* one. He is mine.' At Polly she did not so much as glance. Few people did. It was surprising that Jean darted forward and drew out her chair before he attended to Gwenda, although he shot it out so fast and so far that she almost fell on the floor.

'I really don't think he's all there,' Gwenda said.

She had brought the maps down to breakfast, and said that she thought that they could get to the source of the river that day. It was so beautiful up there in the Auvergne, she said. The air so clear. The flowers so beautiful. At the thought of the flowers, Polly brightened; but there was also the thought of the day ahead, with all the difficulties of the map-reading and Gwenda's making a martyrdom of the driving – though it was she who forced the pace, who was determined to retrace every footstep of that last holiday with her husband. Why she wanted to do this, Polly found a puzzle – especially as that holiday must have been permeated with tragedy. Gwenda had always talked of it a great deal, and she talked of her husband more than Polly could endure. Those trivial repetitions – such as, every morning, '*How* Humphrey loved French bread!' and reminiscences all the way along the road. And there were implications that Polly knew none of the secret joys of matrimony, and would be unlikely ever to learn them. So Polly felt excluded, as well as bored.

Sometimes, alone in her bedroom, she lay for a little while face-down on the bed, upset by vague desires. If the desires were to be loved, she had no face to match to her longing; simply nothing to define her daydreams. 'I want! I just *want*!' she sometimes moaned softly into the pillows.

'Oh, *lazy-bones*!' Gwenda would say, opening the door as she knocked on it. 'Even at my age, I wouldn't dream of lying down in the daytime.' As like as not, she would be on her way downstairs for some of her *violent* exercise. This morning, having mused once more on Humphrey's love of French bread, Gwenda put in her monocle and unfolded a map.

They were breakfasting in the bar, with a view through the open door across the square. It was early in the morning, and children were gathered at the tables outside, waiting for the school bus. The boys smoked, and some of the older girls were playing a game of cards. They were very orderly, though gay, and made a sound like starlings. Gwenda kept glancing up in annoyance, and glaring through her monocle. Polly felt envious of the children.

Madame Devancourt padded past them in her tennis shoes, followed by her son. He bowed again, but she kept her eyes ahead. Presently, Jean appeared outside with a stiff broom and began to sweep between the tables; then he leaned on the broom and talked to some of the children; almost seeming to be one of them, without, for once, his shy or sullen look. Perhaps he too was envious of them, Polly thought.

'Jean, Jean!' Madame Peloux came in in her black overall and called her son's attention to his work, and he shrugged and glowered and began to sweep again.

The school bus came, was filled, and drove off, and there was silence except for the rasping of the broom on the pavement. When he had finished the sweeping, Jean watered the box-shrubs and a sharp, cold smell cut off the heat of the morning for a while.

'Have you packed?' Gwenda asked Polly, knowing that she had not.

As Polly got up, she bumped against the table, and Gwenda looked up sharply and clicked her tongue. Polly, catching Jean's eyes, blushed, ashamed to be rebuked in front of him. He was standing in the doorway, flicking the last drops from the watering-can about the pavement.

As she went upstairs, Polly thought, I'll bet old Humphrey never bumped into things; and she hoped for his sake that he hadn't.

Gwenda paid the bill, then she walked about the courtyard, smoking to soothe herself. The exasperation she felt at always having to wait for Polly was a trembling pain. She hated to wait, and now spent hours of her life doing so. She herself was quick and decisive, always thinking one step ahead. Routine things, like packing, for instance, were so boring that she would get them done with great speed, only to waste time she had saved pacing up and down while Polly dithered.

Jean brought down her case and put it in the boot of the car.

Monsieur Devancourt came out to the garage with his fishing-rods. He stopped to wish Gwenda a pleasant journey, then drove off in his old and dusty Citröen. As Gwenda looked back to the inn for any sign of Polly, she saw old Madame Devancourt, still wearing her hat, staring down at her from a window.

Already the sun was strong. Smells of baking came through the kitchen window, and Gwenda began to long for the cool air of the Auvergne.

At last Jean brought down Polly's suitcase, and Polly followed soon after. Madame Peloux came out from the kitchen, wiping her floury hands on her apron.

As they drove out of the courtyard, Polly thought, 'As

soon as I get to like a place, we have to move on,' and she turned back and waved to Jean, who was staring after them in his vacant way.

But Gwenda was insistent on resuming their journey, on retracing every mile of her holiday with Humphrey. They had to get up to the source and back through Northern France, and there were only ten days left. Then Gwenda must go home to open a garden fête.

'I love this feeling of starting out fresh in the mornings,' she said, as they drove out of the square. 'Humphrey used to say . . .' She slowed down, reaching the main road; the engine stalled, and stopped, and would not start again.

'Oh, drat it,' said Gwenda.

Now the heat poured into the car. While Gwenda tugged at the starter and made her mild, but furious-sounding imprecations, Polly placidly looked at her wild-flower book, as if the hitch did not involve her, and would soon be put right.

Jean, who had watched the car and seen it stop, came running towards them. He opened the bonnet and seemed to take a very grave view. After a while he fetched his friend from the garage. The car was towed away, and Gwenda and Polly decided to return temporarily to the auberge and drink a citron pressé.

'Now, we shall have a job to get to the mountains by this evening,' Gwenda said.

Polly was playing with a cat.

As the day went on, the idea of the mountains receded. Jean carried their suitcases back upstairs, and they unpacked.

'A week at *least*,' Gwenda moaned. 'And if they *say* that, goodness only knows what it might really mean. Stuck in this place.'

'It's quite a *nice* place,' said Polly.

'Yes, but it's not what we planned.'

The car was in the village garage, and a spare part had been telephoned for, and for once there seemed nothing that

Gwenda could do. So she went to lie down, in the heat of the afternoon – the thing she said she never did. Polly, at a loose end, wandered in the orchard, looking for flowers. It was like the afternoons of her childhood, when her mother rested, and she was left to her own devices. In those days, she had felt under a spell. Through an open window she could hear the solid ticking of a grandfather-clock and on the terrace, the peacocks squawking like the sound of rusty shears being forced open. Here there was only the busy noise of the cicadas in the grass.

At the bottom of the orchard, she saw Jean. He was beckoning to her eagerly, and she hurried forward, with a wading motion, through the long grass. He had few words to say – from habit, from gaucherie, from fear of her foreignness. To make up for his dumbness, his gestures were all exaggerated, like Harpo Marx's. They came out of the orchard and crossed the narrow, gritty lane, which was lanced by sunlight striking through birch trees.

With a complete disregard for Polly's bare legs, he took her hand and drew her through looped and tangled brambles, disturbing dozens of small blue butterflies. Polly could hear the stream, but not see it for all the undergrowth. She wondered where they were going, and what all the secrecy and haste and excitement were about. Jean parted some reeds and she could see the stream again. It looked less deep than it was, for it was very clear, and the fat brown stones on its bed seemed near the surface. Jean turned and lifted Polly with his hands round her waist. He swung her down over the bank on to a boulder. It had seemed a sudden, reckless thing to do and her breath was taken away; but she landed quite safely on the boulder, with his large rough hands steadying her.

He became more secretive than ever, carefully drawing aside branches to show to her a part of the stream, caged off by wire netting. The water flowed through the trap, which was full of trout, turning back and forth, and swimming as best they could. So this was his secret? Polly smiled, and he watched her face intently, and when she turned to him and nodded – she knew not why – he put a finger to his lips and narrowed his eyes. To an onlooker they would have seemed like people in a silent movie.

For a moment or two, they stood in contemplation, hypnotized by the slowly moving fish; then, suddenly, with more frantic gestures, Jean dashed off again. He took a spade from a hiding-place under a bush and began to try to thrust it into the earth. Polly turned to watch him with amazement. The earth was hard. He lifted a piece of rough turf and bent to examine the soil, clicking his tongue in disapproval. In spite of the dryness of the earth, he managed, as he dug deeper, to find a few worms. He brought them eagerly to Polly and put them into the palm of her hand, as if they were a handful of precious stones. She recoiled, but he did not notice and, to show her how, he took one of the worms from her and tore it into pieces and threw them to the fish. With a feeling of revulsion, Polly threw her handful suddenly into the trap. Some fell through, others lay on the wire-netting, writhing. She bent down and dipped her hand into the cool water, while Jean poked at the worms with a stick, clicking his tongue in vexation.

'Jean! Jean!' They could hear his mother calling him across the orchard.

He frowned. He watched the trout a little longer, then he seemed to gather himself from a trance, braced himself, and gave his hands to Polly, dragging her clumsily up the bank. 'Jean! Jean!' the voice went on calling, getting shriller. He looped briars carefully over the trap and he and Polly set off.

Madame Peloux was standing in the orchard. She waved a basket at them, for there was some errand for Jean to run – he had to go to the farm to fetch a chicken for dinner. An old boiler, she explained rapidly, aside from Polly.

Polly stood, hesitating, unsure whether to walk on or not. Then, feeling very bold and having composed the sentence in French before she spoke it, she asked if she might go with him to the farm. His face at once lost its sulkiness, and the errand seemed to take on a bright aspect. Madam Peloux stood looking suspiciously after them as they set off.

'What *has* come over you?' Gwenda asked Polly, fearing that she knew. She had found the girl sitting by her bedroom window, studying a phrase-book. It was opened at *Le Marché*.

'You always said I should improve my French,' Polly replied defensively.

'But you never cared to try, did you? Before?'

It was a brilliant early evening, and Gwenda had looked in on her way downstairs. In the garden, the acacias were full of sunlight against the pale-blue sky. Martins and swallows darted about the terra cotta, crenellated outhouse roof, catching, Gwenda hoped, the mosquitoes which otherwise might have plagued her later. There was a smell of lime blossom and honeysuckle and, down below, in the vegetable garden lilies grew like weeds.

'I could stay here for ever, I think,' Polly said glancing across the orchard.

'This was hardly the object of our holiday,' Gwenda said. She was fretful to complete their journey. She talked continually of getting to the source, to the mountains, so infuriatingly near, where she and Humphrey had been so happy. As they were arrested on their travels, there were no fresh sights to discuss, so she talked about Humphrey, and Polly wished that she would not. Gwenda spoke of marriage as if it were something exclusive to herself and her late husband. She referred to past experiences, implying that Polly would never know similar ones.

'Humphrey and I climbed right to the summit,' she said. 'There was an enormous view, and gentians – great patches of gentians.'

'I should love to see gentians,' Polly said.

'Well, I doubt if we shall now,' Gwenda said briskly. 'It's so infuriating. You really ought not to read that small print.

Your nose almost touches the page. So ridiculous. We shall have to see about getting you some spectacles when we get back.'

'I shan't wear them,' Polly said, in a mild but firm voice. Sometimes, quietly, she put her foot down, and then Gwenda let the matter go. It was such a rare occurrence that it did not constitute a threat. All the same, only that morning Polly had insisted on going to the market with Jean, and had left Gwenda at the garage and gone on with him alone. Gwenda was always at the garage, making the same complaints, asking the same questions.

'You'll find you'll come to them in the end,' she said, referring to the spectacles. 'Now do take your head out of that book, there's a dear girl. Let's go down and have a drink. I promised the Devancourts we'd join them.'

Madame Devancourt now seemed warmly disposed to them. She had decided that they were lesbians, and so of no danger to her son. Passing their table at breakfast, the day after the breakdown, the old lady had commiserated with them. She was formal and condescending. By dinner-time, she had warmed a little more; and the following morning had come to them, with her son hovering behind her, to invite them on a drive out in the afternoon. 'Having no car you will see nothing of our country,' she said.

So they had driven out along rutted, dusty lanes to see a small château. It stood high on a slope over the river, bone-white, with black candle-snuffer turrets. Madame Devancourt had the name of a friend to mention, and the housekeeper admitted them. The family was away, and she went ahead from room to room, opening shutters, drawing dust-covers from furniture, lifting drugget from needle-work carpets. There were some portraits, some pieces of tapestry, deers' heads and antlers growing from almost every wall, and a chilly smell from the stone floors. Madame Devancourt and Gwenda exclaimed over everything, drew one another to view this and that treasure or curiosity. Each was impressed by the other's knowledge. Monsieur Devancourt looked out of the windows, and Polly trailed behind, immeasurably bored.

She regretted this new friendship. Gwenda's fluency with French debarred Polly from any part in the conversation – not that she had anything to say. She was frightened of the old lady, and thought her son a pitiful creature. Now they must spend an hour with them sitting under the umbrellas outside the auberge. She took her wild-flower book with her, and looked for a picture of a gentian. '*Gentiane*,' said Jean, pointing at the illustration, when he had set down her drink before her.

'*Oui*,' she said, smiling and blushing.

'*Oui, gentiane*,' he repeated, turning to take an order from another table.

'He will drive me *mad*,' said Gwenda.

Then there was the little commotion of having to get up as Madame Devancourt shuffled out to join them, her son following, carrying her handbag and her cardigan.

At another table came the other sorry pair, the habitueés, the crippled mother and the bitter-faced daughter. Every evening, they sat for twenty minutes in the square. The daughter sipped a drink, and kept propping up her mother. Not a word was spoken. When it was time to go, the daughter stood up in silence and helped her mother to her feet, and then to go slowly across the square. Homewards. Polly tried not to imagine any more – the dreadful ritual of getting mother to bed. All old, she thought, looking round her. Whenever Jean passed by, he nodded his head at her, as if he were saying, 'Ah, yes, you're still there.'

Gwenda, missing nothing, frowned. He continued to madden her through dinner. When he brought the trout, he winked at Polly, collusively.

'One can grow tired even of trout,' Gwenda complained. 'Every evening. I do wish, Polly, you would try to ignore that terrible young man. He is quite oafish. I would have said he winked at you just now, if I could believe it possible.'

She had ordered a bottle of wine to be put on the Devancourts' table – a token of gratitude for their kindness – and now Monsieur Devancourt across the room raised his glass in a courtly gesture, and Madame her glass of water with a shaking hand.

'Very affy,' said Polly in a low voice.

After dinner, the four of them sat in the stuffy little salon, and Gwenda told them stories about her husband.

'Excuse me,' Polly murmured, slipping away suddenly – the very thing Gwenda had been determined she should not do.

In the courtyard, Jean was watering the tubs of geraniums. The air had a delicious smell.

At once, before Gwenda could find an excuse to come after them, he put down the watering-can and they set off across the orchard. Every evening he went to the stream to clean the trout-trap of drifting weeds and sticks and to dig up worms. They said very little – although Polly persevered with a few short sentences, and sometimes Jean pointed at plants and trees and said their name clearly in French, which she obediently repeated.

Although he was clumsy and unpredictable and could not speak a word of her language, Polly felt safe and at home with him. There was never anyone young in her life – neither here nor at home. She liked to go shopping with him in the market. It was the simplest, poorest of markets. Old women sat patiently beside whatever they had for sale – a few broad beans tied in a bundle, a live duck in a basket, lime flowers for tisane, a bucketful of arum lilies or canterbury bells. She and Jean went from one to the other, comparing cheeses, and pressing the bean-pods, and she felt a sense of intimacy, as if they were playing a game of being husband and wife. Nothing Gwenda could say would prevent her from going to the market.

This evening, she helped him to clean the trap, and she fed worms to the fish, having lost her squeamishness. They were as busy and absorbed as children.

Throwing the last worm, she lost her balance on the boulder, and one foot went into the water; but he was there at once to steady her. She was annoyed with herself, wondering how to explain to Gwenda her soaking wet sandal, without revealing the secret of this place.

Jean lifted her up and sat her on the bank.

'I shall stay here for a while,' she said. Perhaps Gwenda would go up to bed early, although more likely not.

He understood her, and sat down beside her, feeling worried, because soon his mother would be calling 'Jean! Jean!' all round the garden – there would be some job to be done.

When they had been together before, there had always been something to be busy about – the marketing, the fish. Now each had only the other one in mind. He sat there staring in front of him, as if he were wondering what on earth to do next, for he had scarcely been allowed five minutes idleness in his life. Then he suddenly had an inspiration. He turned and kissed her suddenly on the side of her face, then, less awkwardly on her forehead. Polly had been kissed only by her mother and elderly relations; but she felt that she knew more about it than Jean. She put her hands behind his head and kissed him very strongly on the mouth. She felt quite faint with delight. But hardly had they had any time to enjoy their kissing, when that far-off, coming and going, mosquito-plaint began – 'Jean! Jean!' – across the orchard.

Until they were in sight of the house, they went hand in hand, saying nothing. Although the kissing was over, something remained – an excitement, a gladness. Something Gwenda, surely, could never have experienced.

That Gwenda guessed something of what had happened was shown by her coldness and huffiness. She had felt awkward, sitting in the salon with the Devancourts. Polly had excused herself so abruptly, and Madame Devancourt kept looking towards the door. Gwenda was glad when, at their usual time, Monsieur Devancourt fetched the draughts board and set out the counters. She watched for a little while, and realized that the son was making stupid mistakes so that his mother could win. Then, hearing Madame Peloux outside calling for Jean, Gwenda got up uneasily, and said that she was going to have an early night. She went upstairs and threw open the window, regardless of mosquitoes.

Polly and Jean were coming back across the orchard. Gwenda began to shake violently, and moved back a few steps from the window. Jean answered his mother, but did not say a word to Polly, not even when she turned away from him to enter the house.

Gwenda was so unpleasantly disturbed that she felt unable to face Polly, and dreaded her coming to say good night. But she did not come. The footsteps stopped at the next room, and Gwenda heard the door open, and then shut. This was something that had never happened before. There were too many things happening for the first time. Gwenda lay in bed worrying about them, and she slept badly.

At breakfast, nothing was right. She snapped at Jean for slopping the coffee, she complained that the butter was rancid, and she found every word that Polly said in French excruciating. 'Your command of the language grows as fast as your accent deteriorates.' She preferred the days when Polly did not try, and had no reason for doing so. 'Whatever must the Devancourts think? They must wonder where on earth you came by such an accent.'

'It's not *for* them to wonder,' Polly said calmly. 'They can't speak a *word* of English.'

She *was* calm. She was *too* calm, Gwenda decided. And Jean did not look at her this morning, nor she at him. It seemed to Gwenda that they no longer felt they needed to.

'Oh, *damn* the car,' she suddenly said.

Polly looked a little surprised, but said nothing.

'I think I'll have a look round the market this morning,' Gwenda said casually.

The three of them later set off, and there was only a brief chance to make an assignation, when Gwenda almost instinctively paused to look at a terrine on a stall.

The friendship with the Devancourts played into Polly's hands. Just at the right moment of the afternoon, Madame Devancourt came downstairs with a photograph-album to show Gwenda her collection of photographs of great houses, all to be gone over and explained in detail, trapping Gwenda until she thought that she would scream. Monsieur Devancourt was attending to his fishing-tackle, so the two women were left alone, sitting in the stuffy salon. It was too hot to go out of doors, Madame Devancourt said.

Polly, who had gone into the lavatory to try to plan her escape, saw the delightful sight of Gwenda with the album on her knees and Madame Devancourt leaning over, pointing at a photograph with a shaking finger. She slipped away without being seen. Jean, whose slack time it was, was waiting for her by the trout-trap. He pulled briars and bracken round them, like a nest and, without much being said, made love to her.

The old lady smelled of camphor and lavender. She leant so close that Gwenda almost choked. Sometimes little flecks of spit fell on the pages of the album, and were quickly wiped away with the purple handkerchief. Gwenda tried to turn the pages quickly, but this would not do; for every coign and battlement and drawbridge had to be explained.

At last Monsieur Devancourt interrupted them. He had finished with his fishing-tackle and had come to take them for a little drive. Where was Mademoiselle Polly, he wondered. Gwenda flushed, and said that she must be writing letters in her room; and she excused herself from the outing, having a headache, she explained.

When they had gone, Gwenda walked up and down the garden path. She strutted, with legs rather apart, like a starling. She listened and looked about her. But there were no voices. It was a hot, humming afternoon. The Devancourts' car went off, and then there was nothing but the sound of insects, and hardly a leaf moved.

'Her mother!' Gwenda kept saying to herself. 'What would her mother think?'

It was a real headache she had, and the sun was making it much worse. It drove her inside – up to the vantage-point of her bedroom window.

It was a long time before she saw Polly coming back across the orchard. She walked slowly and was alone. But that was only a ruse, a piece of trickery, Gwenda was sure.

She leaned out of the window and called to her.

Polly seemed to come unwillingly, and stood hesitating at Gwenda's door.

'Where have you been?'

'For a walk.'

'With that dreadful loutish youth.'

Polly pressed her lips together.

'He's not even ...' Gwenda shrugged and turned aside; and after a few moments in which nothing else was said, Polly went quietly to her own room. Although she foresaw all the agonizing awkwardness of the rest of the holiday – even, vaguely, of the rest of her life (Gwenda going on being huffy in Surrey) – she dismissed its importance. She stood before the looking-glass, combing her hair dreamily, staring at her freckled face with its band of sun-burn across the forehead. It was she now, she decided, who had something exclusively her own, and it seemed to her that Gwenda had nothing – for even her memories were threadbare.

In the night, just before dawn, Gwenda woke up. Something had disturbed her, and she lay listening. There was silence, save for far-away cow-bells occasionally heard. Then a floor-board creaked on the landing, and another. There was a gentle tapping on a bedroom door, and whispering.

She felt very cold, and sick, and deceived. She groped for her watch and peered at its luminous dial. It was nearly five o'clock. There was no real light in the sky, but perhaps a lessening of darkness.

Boards now creaked quite heavily along the passage, down the stairs. Gwenda got out of bed and went to the window, gently easing the shutters apart. As she did so, she heard an outside door open, and then a man's voice, speaking in low tones just below her. As her eyes grew used to the dark, she could make out two figures. After a moment, they moved off towards the courtyard, and she could see then that they were Jean and Monsieur Devancourt, both carrying fishing-rods. After a while, she heard the car starting up. It drove away, and she listened to it fading into the distance. Then the church clock struck five.

She left the shutters opened, and got back into bed. The sky slowly lightened, and she turned about heavily on the rough, darned sheets, longing for day to come so that she could get on with it, hasten through it. She searched her mind for plans for escaping from this hated place, and, faced with all the complications, found none.

At breakfast, Gwenda was tired and silent. She seemed to brood over her coffee, staring before her, the drooping lines of her face deeper than ever. Monsieur Devancourt and Jean returned, having caught a large pike. Jean quickly slipped on a white jacket and brought fresh coffee. Monsieur Devancourt joined his mother, and peeled her orange for her, was full of simple triumph at his successful expedition, and now wanted nothing but to devote the rest of the day to her. They discussed their plans with great pleasure.

As usual, Madame Devancourt stopped on her way past Gwenda's and Polly's table.

'How early a riser would it be possible for you to be?' she asked. She seemed playful, like a child with a secret. She hardly waited for Gwenda's reply. 'Then,' she went on, 'we have a little plan, Louis and I. We know your disappointment at not reaching the source of the river, and we think that if we can start early tomorrow we can make the journey and spend the following night en route. It would give us great pleasure. How does it strike you?'

It struck Gwenda very well, and she said so. She brightened at once. Polly, who never understood what Madame Devancourt said, had not tried to listen. When it was explained to her, she was appalled, and too artless to hide the fact. Gwenda touched her foot under the table to bring her to her senses; but she could only stammer her thanks, while looking quite dismayed.

'But it's dreadful for *me*,' she complained to Gwenda afterwards. 'I can't understand a single word they say. To have a long drive like that with them!'

She knew that she would have to go. She was not strong enough to resist Gwenda over this. After a while she forgot what was hanging over her. She was living in the present, and it was time to go to market with Jean. Gwenda, more relaxed now, let them go alone, while she visited the garage and made another fuss.

The next day, they left very early. Jean was up before them and brought them coffee and bread. It was a strange, cold dawn, and they moved about quietly, with lowered voices, putting things into the boot of the car. At the last moment, Polly found she had forgotten her wild-flower book and had to get out of the car and go and find it. It was her only solace – and such a small one to her in her altered life – that she might see gentians growing in the mountains. Jean stood ready to open the car door for her when she returned. His eyes rested mournfully upon her. As they drove off, she could see him standing there, staring after her, looking sulky.

Madame Devancourt was quite talkative that morning. She sat in front beside her son, and half turned her wedge-shaped face back towards Gwenda. Polly she completely ignored. She thought her an imbecile and wondered that Gwenda had not found a more intelligent and presentable partner. It seemed to her that they were not so very much in love, though in such cases, she found it difficult to tell.

They stopped for lunch at an inn full of memories for Gwenda. She was delighted. Her spirits had been rising all morning, as they climbed higher into the colder air. She became animated, and infected Madame Devancourt with her liveliness. Both had such recollections – and all along the route the two widows exchanged them. La Bourboule! Le Mont-Dore! There were changes to be noted. Yet so much had remained the same. Monsieur Devancourt listened to them as he drove, smiling to see his mother so gay. It was unusual for her to have feminine companionship, and it seemed to do her good. Polly stared at the wild flowers along the way. She was obviously not allowed to stop to gather them. Monsieur Devancourt sometimes addressed a remark to her and then she started out of her dreams and became confused, and Gwenda had to rescue her.

After lunch, they went on to the source. The river they had driven beside became, at last, a thin fast trickle down the mountainside. The road ended. They got out of the car and felt the air cold on their faces, and Polly looked about for flowers. The gentians were higher up, Gwenda told her, and she said that she for one was determined to climb to the summit, as she and Humphrey had done. They could be taken nearly there in the funicular.

Madame Devancourt declined. She would sit in the car and wait for them, and be quite happy reading her novel, she explained.

'Your mother is charming,' Gwenda told Monsieur Devancourt as they waited for the lift to come down.

'It is altogether a charming day,' he said.

As they were hauled up by the cable-car, Polly, although dizzy, peered down at the rocks for flowers. She saw miniature daffodils, drifts of white anemones, and then, in a crevice, a patch of gentians. The funicular swung high above them and came to a stop.

This much higher up, it was windy. Strands of hair kept lashing her cheeks. She hated the wind, and she hated being so high. Above them, at the top of a zig-zagging path, she could see two tiny figures waving from the highest rock.

'I shouldn't like to go up there,' she said to Gwenda.

'But that's why we've come,' Gwenda said with a tone of scorn. 'Humphrey . . .' Then she changed her mind about what she was going to say. She would climb to the summit alone with Monsieur Devancourt and say not a word about her husband all the way.

Polly, on this lower slope was quite content to scramble about and pick flowers. The tiny daffodils were exquisite, and there were varieties she could not classify until she got back to the car and found them in her book. But she could find no gentians. They seemed to grow in rockier parts. Here, there was only shabby, wind-bitten grass and patches of dirty snow. Barbed-wire ran along the edge of the ridge. Beyond it rocks went sheer down to the valley.

From the summit, Gwenda and Monsieur Devancourt, rather out of breath paused triumphantly and looked about them at the wide view. They could see Polly below, darting like a child or a bee, from one flower to another, and they called to her, but their voices were snatched out of their throats by the wind.

Then Gwenda began to shout in earnest, for she could see that Polly was trying to crawl under the barbed wire at the edge of a steep drop. She was lying on her stomach, reaching for something. Gwenda and Monsieur Devancourt called out in warning and began to scramble down the slippery path as quickly as they could. Before they could come within Polly's hearing, there was a dreadful rushing noise of bouncing and cascading scree, of rocks dropping with an echo upon other rocks. The noise continued long after Polly had disappeared and Gwenda and Monsieur Devancourt had come to the newly-opened fissure. Beside it was a handful of flowers, and a piece of gentian-blue chocolate-paper which Polly must have been reaching for.

Monsieur Devancourt had been a tower of strength. He

had interviewed police officials and undertakers, intercepted newspaper-men, booked the flight home, arranged about the coffin, sent telegrams, and brought Gwenda back to Selonac to pack the cases. And every now and then he bewailed the fact that the tragic excursion had been his idea.

Gwenda was stunned, rather than grief-stricken. She leaned on his kindness. She let him do everything for her.

Madame Devancourt now seemed to have withdrawn. Her son's solicitude was irksome and disturbing, and looks of suspicion were cast on him and Gwenda. The episode had been distasteful, encroaching – and she had had enough of her, this Englishwoman, with her demanding ways. Instead of taking command, as one of her kind should have done, she had clung to a man like any silly girl.

'I can never say "thank you" enough,' Gwenda said. She had come to them in the salon to bid them good-bye. 'When you come to England, I hope you will stay with me, in my house in Surrey.'

Madame Devancourt nodded forbiddingly; but Gwenda hardly noticed. In her mind, she was introducing Monsieur Devancourt – he had asked her to call him 'Louis' – to her friends. 'Do you play bridge?' she very nearly asked him; but she stopped herself in time. She shook hands. Once more Louis blamed himself for Polly's death, and his mother clicked her tongue impatiently.

Out in the courtyard, the car was waiting – ready at last; ready too late – and Jean was packing the cases into the boot. Gwenda had forgotten all about him. Madame Peloux stood by to wish her 'Bon Voyage'.

She looked into her bag for a tip, and advanced with it folded in her hand, ready to slip it into Jean's. He slammed down the lid of the boot and, as Gwenda came up to him, he turned sulkily aside, and walked away.

His face was swollen; he made a blubbering noise, like a miserable child and, going faster and faster, made off across the orchard.

'Ah, Jean! Jean!' his mother said, with a sigh and a shake of her head, looking after him.

Gwenda got into the car. It started perfectly. She waved to Madame Peloux and to Louis Devancourt, who had come out of the inn to watch her go, and drove away, towards the airport.

Dan Jacobson

Another Day

I was lying in the shade of a peach tree that grew to the side of the lawn. Behind me sprawled our house, with its broad red stoep, its white pillars and white wooden shutters. Overhead, above the thin, tapering leaves of the peach tree, was the clear sky. It was a Sunday morning: one of the vacant, interminable, never-changing Sunday mornings of childhood. My parents were out of the house, but I could hear the African servants talking idly to one another in the backyard. The air was warm; a contrasting coolness rose from the grass underneath me; in my nostrils was the faint, bitter, almond-like scent of the peach leaves. Every sensation I was conscious of seemed to contribute to the wide, full stillness of the day; each was part of its calm. I held a book in my hands, but I wasn't reading it.

I was roused by a strange rumbling noise coming from the road. The noise grew louder; within the rumble I could hear the squeak of metal, the crunch of sand or gravel against the tar of the road. Drawn by curiosity, I went to the fence and looked outside.

I was shocked to see what had broken into the morning's suburban silence. The noise I had heard was that of a funeral procession. But what a funeral procession! What a cortège of mourners! What a hearse! On a flat, wooden two-wheeled barrow of the kind used to carry vegetables and coops of chickens in the market square, a metal frame had been erected, from which there hung a canopy of a few black strips of cloth. Beneath this wretched canopy, naked on the planks of the barrow, rested a small coffin. As the wheels turned, metal rims grating on the tar, the barrow shook at every joint; and the coffin on it shook too.

The coffin was that of a child. It was a plain wooden box without handles or ornament of any kind. At its corners, roughly sawn, the heads of a few nails shone brightly. The child in the coffin must have been even younger than I was at the time: the box wasn't more than three feet long. Next to it, on the planks, there lay a spade.

The barrow was level with me; then it had gone by. None of the three people following it had noticed me. The man pushing the barrow was a young, strongly built African dressed in a pair of shorts and striped cotton shirt. His head was bare, and so were his feet. The calf-muscles of each leg bunched as he took his strides off the balls of his feet, leaning forward slightly against the barrow. His head was lowered, and from his mouth there came a wordless, tuneless chant. Behind him walked two African women, long dresses trailing around their ankles, and fringed shawls about their shoulders and over their heads. They both clutched their shawls together with their hands in front of their mouths, so that their faces were veiled, hidden.

No one else was in the street; no one else seemed to be standing in any of the gardens to watch the procession go by. On an impulse, I went to the gate and began to follow them.

Groaning and rumbling, the barrow went down the road. We covered the distance of one block, a second, a third. Here and there someone working in his garden paused for a moment to stare, or an African walking up the road stopped, shook his head, and went on. No one seemed to associate me with the group. I followed under a compulsion I did not understand but could not disobey, unable to take my eyes off the powerful legs of the man pushing the barrow, the bowed heads of the women, and the light, shaking box that contained the corpse of a child younger than myself.

We passed a police station and some small shops. The road descended into a subway and passed under the railway lines. Beyond the railway the road was no longer tarred; the area was an outright slum, inhabited by poor-whites and Cape Coloureds, bordered by acres upon acres of the mine-dumps which lay all around the outskirts of our town. The dumps were enclosed within a fierce barbed-wire fence, twelve feet high. The group with the barrow turned and followed a dusty, pitted road that ran parallel to the railway lines. Soon there were no houses around us at all. On one side were the railway lines, on the other the barbed-wire and the mine-dumps.

I thought I knew where we were going. About a mile farther down the road there was an African 'location', thrust down on a flat stretch of ground, where the mining company's wire curved away from the railway. However, when the group came to a fork in the road, only the two women went straight on to the location; the man pushed the barrow some way down the road to the left before halting and throwing himself down in the shade of a little camel-thorn tree that grew to the side of the road. He left the barrow with the coffin on it standing in the sun. The women were soon lost to sight in the confusion of rust-coloured, dust-coloured shacks that stretched away indistinguishably across the bare, level earth. In the strong sunlight the location looked vast but insubstantial.

Hesitantly, hearing the sound of my own footsteps on the road and watching my own shadow in front of me, I approached the man. Only when I was within a few feet of him did I look up. He had drawn himself up at my approach; he was sitting with his knees raised in front of his chest and his arms behind him, propping up his body. He smiled cheerfully at me. His teeth were white, his skin smooth, his face broad. Over each eye there was a protuberance of bone which might have given his face an angry, lowering aspect if his expression had not been so amused. His eyes seemed to peep slyly at me under his heavy brows.

'What are you looking for?' he asked me, in Afrikaans. His voice was deep, and had an idle, teasing note to it.

I could not answer him. Yet it seemed that he knew what I wanted, and was ready to tell me all he could. He turned his head away from me and looked at the coffin, wrinkling his brow against the brightness of the sunlight beyond the shadow in which he lay.

'The little boy in there – he had a sickness in his chest. They fetch his *ouma*, the grandmother, now. Then we go to the graveyard.'

He held up a single dust-stained finger. 'I do all the work for a pound. Just one pound, and I make the coffin, and I take it where they want me to, and I dig the hole also.'

He fell silent, still regarding me from under his brows, half-threatening, half-quizzical. Then he said: 'You want to look inside? Come!' And he rose swiftly on the word.

I turned and ran. Behind me I heard the man laughing; then a scurry of footsteps in the sand. He was coming after me. Sickeningly, the earth seemed to turn across all its width, like a great, flat, pallid wheel; I could not keep my balance on it. I fell, and looked up. His smiling face was over me.

'Don't run away,' he said. His hands grasped me gently. I was sure I was going to die. Death itself stood over me, determined to punish my curiosity by satisfying it utterly. What had happened to that other child was going to happen to me. I was going to learn all that he had learned.

I don't remember the man letting go of me, or hearing his footsteps retreating from me. All I knew when I opened my eyes was that the man's face was no longer between me and the sky. I did not look where he had gone. I got to my feet and took a few paces, but felt too weak and unsteady to go on. There was a ditch to the side of the road, and I crept into it. How long I lay there, with my head on my arms and my eyes closed, I do not know. When at last I stood up, I found that the man and his barrow were gone. I also found, without surprise, that having come so far I felt I must go on.

I could see the wheel tracks that the barrow had left in the sand and I began to follow them. A car passed me, with a swirl of dust at its tyres, and I saw the people in it looking at me curiously. I went on walking. To the left, the barbed-wire fence ran straight, the dumps of earth lying empty behind it. On the right, almost as bare of vegetation as the dumps, was a stretch of veld where a few piccanins were playing with a ball. The spaces around them made their figures look tiny. Then I saw the location's cemetery.

It looked much like the veld where the piccanins were playing, only its surface was more irregular, broken by innumerable little mounds of earth. There was no fence around it. From hundreds of the mounds there gleamed little points of light: reflections from the jam tins which were used to hold the flowers brought by mourners. There were only a few formal tombstones to be seen; there were more wooden crosses, some of them tilted at angles; there were many strips of corrugated iron thrust upright into the ground, with names painted on them. Some of the graves had their borders carefully marked out by small boulders laid in rows on the ground. But most of them were quite without adornment, identification, or demarcation of any kind. It was impossible to tell where each ended or began. There was not a tree, not even a bush, anywhere. Among all the low mounds and humps of earth, the people I was looking for stood out distinctly. There were three women, and the man working with a spade.

The women stood aside from the man, next to the barrow with the coffin on it. They did not seem to be weeping; merely watching and waiting. When the hole was a few feet deep – the rim of it came to the man's waist when he stood in it – he clambered out, wiped his brow, and simply picked up the coffin and carried it in his arms to the grave, holding it in front of his chest. The women cried out briefly, then were silent. The man slid the coffin, end foremost, into the grave and climbed in after it to lay it flat. A moment later he had climbed out again and had set about shovelling the earth inside the hole, working very fast.

The women waited until he had done. Then they turned and began walking towards the location, taking a short cut across the veld. The man, alone once more, pushed the empty barrow to the road, where I was standing. The going was difficult for him, among the graves, and it took him some time to draw near.

Eventually he reached the road. He blew out his breath noisily and smiled. In his deep, mocking voice he said, 'Another time.' He pointed a finger at me and shook it. 'Another day.'

I began walking home, ahead of him. All the way home I heard the rumble of the barrow behind me. At the gate of the house I stood and watched the man go past; I knew he was conscious of me, but he did not look in my direction. He did not need to. His head was lowered, and from his lips there came that tuneless, wordless chant I had heard before. The muscles of his legs quivered with every long stride he took.

Dan Jacobson

Through the Wilderness

I met Boaz, the Israelite, at a time when I was doing nothing. I was idle, stagnant, dead still.

This was just after my twentieth birthday, when I should have been at my most energetic, restless, and ambitious. Or so I used to tell myself. Instead, I was stuck fast, as if forever, in my hometown, Lyndhurst, in South Africa. Not long before I had excitedly made my plans to go to Europe, to go to Israel, to travel as far as I could into the waiting world. But having been compelled to cancel those plans just a few days before I had been due to leave, I remained at home, like someone in a thrall, unable to move without sufficient energy even to want to do so.

I suppose I'm exaggerating a little when I say that I was doing nothing. There were three things which I did regularly, and which could possibly be called work. At least they were activities of a kind. I went to the hospital every day to visit my father. I took Hebrew lessons three times a week. I went once a week to the farm my father owned, to deliver rations to the 'boys' and to count the sheep.

2

The sheep-counting was something of a farce. Have you ever tried to count a flock of two hundred-odd sheep being driven in a cloud of dust from one *kraal* to another adjacent to it, through a narrow gate? Tried without being practised at it, I mean? I was town-born and bred (small town, admittedly, but town nevertheless); I had just spent three years at the university in Johannesburg; I was no farm boy, no cattleman, no shepherd.

Driven by two diminutive, barefooted herd boys, who waved large sticks over their heads and yelled fiercely in Tswana and Afrikaans, the sheep milled together, ran in every direction, bleated furiously, and came running in bunches through the gate, where I stood with Piet, the herd boys' father, each of us to one side. We counted them as they ran, their woolly coats quivering, their eyes ablaze with terror, their foolish, triangular mouths open. The dust they raised in the air was green and acrid, made of the dung they had dropped on previous occasions.

Invariably, at the end of each counting there was a discrepancy between the figure I had arrived at and the figure given to me by Piet. Invariably, my figure was somewhat lower than his. Each of us having announced his figure, an embarrassed pause would follow.

A question hung unspoken in that silence: Was Piet stealing the sheep? It was a question I found impossible to answer. If I was right one week in finding the total to be two hundred and twenty-five, say, then surely I was wrong the next week in finding it to be two hundred and forty-five. Or was I? What was there to stop Piet, after a larger than usual depredation, from insinuating ten or twenty of his own sheep into my father's flock when the time came for them to be counted? For he did have a small flock of his own, of which he was a most attentive keeper, about which he bargained and bickered and came to obscure arrangements with Africans on neighbouring farms. I couldn't tell his sheep from any other; they were all the same black-headed Persian type, with dusty off-white bodies; none had been branded or dyed distinctively.

Piet was gentle with me, but unyielding. He would clear his throat, breaking the silence between us; he would gesture soothingly with the hand that clutched the bowl of the small, unlit pipe he almost invariably carried. He was a slight, untalkative, middle-aged man, with a mouth pursed forward in an expression of melancholy, dogged doubt; around his mouth, on both sides, there ran two deep wrinkles, like a pair of elongated parentheses. He looked reflective, sceptical, and somehow urban; his face might have been that of a lawyer, or a petty shopkeeper perhaps, a seller of stationery and stamps. But he was a shepherd, nothing more, and his clothes were almost as ragged as those of his children. His shirt was a mere accumulation of patches; his shoes were so hard, large, and cracked, they might have been made of unseasoned timber. I was pretty sure he put on those shoes only in honour of my visits, and went around barefoot the rest of the time. On his head he wore a brown woollen cap with an implausible pom-pom.

'Nee, my baas,' he might say. *'Twee honderd drie en dertig.'*

Two hundred and thirty-three. He had counted them, and that was his total. I had counted and got two hundred and twenty-seven. So this week the discrepancy was only six. Last week it had been nineteen. The week before it had been fourteen. What was the truth? Would I never know it? What was I going to do now?

I did what I always did: I stared hard at Piet, who met my gaze with a look of dutiful, dignified submission. Pouting, head drooping, pompom hanging forward, he waited for me to pronounce judgement. Sometimes I said we should count the sheep all over again, which we would do amid renewed dust and confusion, with results as unsatisfactory as before. More often I said that we would count them more carefully, more slowly, next time. Then we would leave, while the sheep, still protesting, would be driven out of the *kraal* and down the slope to the grazing lands.

They had more than three thousand acres to graze in, those sheep. Three thousand acres of pale grass, stunted black camelthorn trees, and innumerable nipple-shaped, knee-high antheaps of dried earth; the whole area being divided by wire fences into 'camps', with an iron windmill and an iron water tank in each one. You could see every windmill and tank, you could see all three thousand acres, and God knows how many hundreds of thousands of acres beyond – belonging to Pope, to Van Aswegan, to Huyssteen, to Jaap Burger, to the Lyndhurst General Mining and Exploration Company – from the farmhouse where I always parked the car. Behind the farmhouse there was a ridge of *koppies* and the slight elevation on which the house stood was enough to give a view that stretched all the way I had come. The only irregularity on the horizon were the mine-dumps of Lyndhurst, sixteen miles away. From there the white dirt road ran through one farm after another; past the ridge behind the farmhouse it was lost to sight. Out of curiosity I had once followed it beyond the farm, and had found that it arrived eventually at a miserable, shadeless huddle of iron-roofed buildings called Platkop, thirty miles further on.

It was called, for some reason, the Samarian Road. Why Samarian? What had it to do with Samaria? None of the farms along its route was named Samaria, so far as I knew.

Anyway, that was the road, that was the view, from the sagging wire fence that separated the sand of the veld from the sand of the farmhouse 'garden'. The house itself was a low iron-roofed building, whitewashed inside and out, divided into four small rooms. The only item of furniture still in it was a hat-stand. A real, elaborate, varnished hat-stand, with fierce antlers for hats arching out of a kind of node near the top, and two rings of wood around its lower half, to contain umbrellas. Umbrellas? In that climate? I used to go into the house to see that everything was in order. 'Everything' was invariably 'in order', though I found every time I went in that more whitewash had flaked from the walls and that more and more insects appeared to be occupying the place. Black and yellow striped hornets made their nests plumb against the walls, spiders spun their webs in corners, ants hoarded their food in nests between floorboards. Overhead, between the iron roof and the buckled beaverboard ceiling, I could hear faint scurryings and crepitations – birds, perhaps, or mice, were nesting there.

Everything, I repeat, was in order. The only disorder, the only visible movement in the house was that of the motes of dust that swarmed and twinkled in columns of sunlight coming in through the windows. The walls sent off a cloud of white dust if I struck them with the palms of my hands, and I often did it, partly for the sake of seeing the dust fly, and partly for the sake of the flat, echoless sound, where no other sound was. Then I would go out. The veld always surprised me, when I came out: the house was so cramped and meagre, the veld so very large. Yet in point of life there didn't seem to be all that much to choose between them.

But, waiting around the car, would be Piet and his family, and Kagisho and his family. Kagisho, the other 'boy', Piet's assistant, was many years older than Piet; he was bent, frail, and Bushman-like in appearance, with a skin that had a queer reddish or golden tint. Around them sprawled, squatted, and slept their many children. I say slept because that's what the youngest children were doing, slung in fringed shawls on their mothers' backs. I would have thought both women to have passed the childbearing age; but they obviously had not. For that matter, I would have thought Kagisho to be beyond the child-propagating age. But perhaps he had handed his wife over to Piet with the same alacrity he showed when I once heard Piet ask him to hand over the pay I had just given him.

I paid Piet and Kagisho once a month; every week each family was given so much mealie meal, so much sugar, so much tea, so much tobacco. In addition I sometimes off-loaded salt or sulphur or bonemeal for the sheep. Whether or not the sheep ever got these rations I do not know. And there were usually one or two other items that Piet had asked me to get the previous week – a bottle of cough mixture for one of his children, or some kaffircorn malt which he used to brew his own beer. I always brought the children packets of barley-sugar, which each came up in turn to receive, in cupped hands. They thanked me formally for these. Once when one of them forgot to do so he was reminded by Piet, who sent the delinquent tumbling with a single, savage blow across the back of the head.

So my 'work' on the farm would be over. I'd tell Piet to expect me at the same time the next week, and get into the car. The women would smile and bob their heads, hands clutching their long skirts; the children would wave; Piet would send *groete* – greetings – to the *oubaas* – my father; Kagisho, who was always both industrious and ineffectual in the off-loading, would give a sudden start as though he too feared a blow from Piet, and hastily send his *groete*, as well, to the *oubaas*. Somewhere along the road I'd pass the sheep on the way to the particular camp they were grazing in, and I'd wave to the solitary boy herding them. And so, home.

There were just two ways of going home: one was very fast, the other very slow. It was purely a matter of mood which way I did the journey; it never made a difference to anyone else. I had no appointments to keep. When I travelled fast, my ambition was to cover the sixteen miles between the farm and town in fifteen minutes. This was not at all easy to do on an ill-kept, corrugated dirt road, which curved zealously around every clump of thornbushes, and which was interrupted at least half-a-dozen times by narrow cattle-grids. Many of the curves were almost blind, where the thornbushes grew particularly thickly, and all of them were made trickier by the drifts of sand at their sides. I had some narrow escapes on that road, and so did the oncoming motorists I sometimes found myself confronting in a cloud of dust, to the sound of blaring, astonished horns and skidding tyres.

When I went slowly I'd drive as slowly as I could in top gear, until the car began to stall, then I'd change down into second and do the same; then the same in first. I'd accelerate to seventy miles an hour, switch off the ignition, and see how far the car would go before coming to a halt. I would turn the car round so that it faced the farm again, put it into reverse, and drive backwards for a couple of miles. Many times I simply stopped the car at the side of the road, walked a little way into the veld, and lay down on the sand and tufts of grass, shielding my eyes from the sun and looking straight up into the blue sky until it swam with a multitude of tiny, squirming shapes that were dark and bright at the same time. Or I stared at a particular thornbush, trying to impress it so firmly on my mind that I would be able to visualize it in every detail an hour later, when I would be back in Lyndhurst. But I found that usually it was something nearby that I hadn't been concentrating on, seeing only out of the corner of my eye, which I would really remember: the knobbly, hard surface of an antheap, or a particular tuft of grass, or the bland, flat face of a locust, its eyes like tiny beads pasted on, which had jumped on to my trouser leg.

I was seldom disturbed by anything other than insects. A car, or some solitary African on foot or on a bicycle, might pass on the road; I daresay they were curious about the empty car standing on the roadside, but insufficiently so ever to come and look for me. I was on my own, surrounded by a flat, blank vacancy of sky and veld, a world of pale colours and strong light. It was abysmally dull, mull, motionless, limitless, meaningless.

Eventually I would drive on to meet the main tarred road, where the view opened out on the town itself: low iron roofs, which always looked black in the strong sunlight; a group of taller buildings in the town centre, also black; some trees, the same; mine dumps of green sand in a rough circle around the entire scatter of the place. I used to skirt the town, going home along a by-pass road which had pairs of tram-tracks running parallel to it, for some distance, before they branched off into the veld, making for no visible destination at all. Poles, no longer carrying cables, arched over the tracks. God knows when they had been laid down, and with what expectations. The expectations had clearly not been fulfilled, but the tracks and poles still marched bravely and aimlessly across the bare veld, under the wide sky.

3

So much for my 'work' on the farm. As for the Hebrew lessons . . .

All the attempts that had been made in my childhood to teach me Hebrew had ended in failure. I had been determinded that they should. For obvious reasons, I had associated the Hebrew language with being alien, set apart, exposed; implicated in what I was convinced at an early age was a continuing, unendurable history of suffering and impotence; involved with a religion in whose rituals I could find no grace, no power, no meaning, and that had no connexion I could discern with the dusty, modern mining town in South Africa in which I was growing up. I can still remember how intensely I hated the very pictures in the books from which we had been taught Hebrew. They were old books, who knew how old, and the pictures in them were ugly, small, cramped, full of thick black lines. The boys who appeared in the pictures were physically puny, dressed in skullcaps, long jackets, and grotesque knickerbockers; they had earlocks hanging from their temples; they were imprisoned in rooms that looked both over-furnished and poverty-stricken; they sat in devout, learning postures, receiving instruction from bearded rabbis or winding their phylacteries around their arms. I cannot describe the claustrophobia, the anguish of embarrassment and distaste, they roused in me. Was I learning Hebrew to become like one of those boys? Was that the prize? I would sooner have died.

So I hadn't learned much more than the script and a handful of words and constructions in all the years I attended, or failed to attend, the classes conducted in the synagogue-hall by Mr Saltzmann, the local community's ritual slaughterer, ritual circumciser, and instructor to the youth. I had never learned to understand the prayers that I heard sung, muttered, or sighed in the synagogue. I had never read any of the volumes in Hebrew that filled the bottom row of the big bookcase in our living-room: the Bible and commentaries on the Bible, the works of Yehuda Halevi and Ibn Gabirol, the collected poems of moderns like Bialik and Tchernichowsky, a translation of Graetz's *History* in four volumes. Those books, imposingly bound in imitation leather, and in a peculiarly hairy green cloth, and in multi-coloured marbled boards, were my parents', never mine.

Yet – or hence – here I was, a Zionist now, learning Hebrew once again. And what was more, learning it from the same Mr Saltzmann who had tried so hard to teach it to me in my childhood. Three times a week we sat at the big table in the dining room, surrounded by sideboards with mahogany roses worked all over them, mirrors in heavy mahogany frames, a clock in a glass and mahogany case five feet tall and complete with a pendulum, which unfortunately did not work. When we looked up from our books we stared into an elaborate marble fireplace, and a mantel that incorporated a melancholy lithograph of three sheepdogs in a hut somewhere in Scotland. One could tell that the hut was in Scotland because the largest of the dogs was standing guard over a plaid and a tam o'shanter, presumably the property of the shepherd, who was nowhere to be seen. His absence, I might say, lent a touch of drama to the picture which it otherwise sadly lacked.

Inevitably, in these surroundings, so intimately familiar to me that in recollection they seem to belong to an inner world of dream rather than to any external world of fact, I got to know Mr Saltzmann far better than I ever had as a child. With his bitten nails, his lined brow, his shoulders of unequal height, his unexpectedly strong head of wavy, silver hair, his pallid skin, he looked exactly as he had years before. Then I had thought of him only as a threat and a bore; now I came to know him as an assiduous reader of newspapers, as a rather dissatisfied husband and family man, as a small-scale speculator in real estate, as an enthusiast for certain finer points of Hebrew grammar. We discussed, in a desultory, subdued way, such topics as the meaning of life, the prospects of an after-life, the future of the State of Israel, and the relation between science and religion. On all these subjects I thought Mr Saltzmann surprisingly cautious, in view of the position he held in the community. He did not seem to know just where he stood. Yet I did not feel it would have been right to accuse him of insincerity when he led the prayers in synagogue, or when he cut the throats of chickens, cattle, and sheep in the ritually prescribed manner. Far from it. In holding fast to his orthodoxy Mr Saltzmann seemed to me as sincere and singleminded about what he was doing as a man washed overboard in the middle of the ocean would be in clutching at a spar. If you were to be so heartless as to ask such a man if he 'believed' in his spar, you would get the same kind of answer that Mr Saltzmann gave to me. What else was there? Why throw it away? Who can be so choosy?

But we didn't spend all our time in conversation; we did pay some attention to our books. The book we used chiefly had been published by the Zionist Organization of America, and was as modern and secular as it possibly could have been. In simple Hebrew it described the adventures of the family Cohen, who sailed one day on a ship to Palestine, and who were so enchanted by everything they saw that they decided to settle there without further ado. On the whole these Cohens were a devoted but charmless family, easily excited into fits of enthusiasm and much given to explaining things to one another. By the end of the book I was up to everything they did and said; I understood their laborious conversations and their few, feeble jokes. In fact, by the time I'd finished the book I was beginning to fancy that already I knew more about the Hebrew language than the poor Cohens ever would; that I had already grasped something of its inner spirit, of its harshness, its archaic severity and compression, its lack of sinuosity, all of which were illustrated for me not just in its sounds and constructions but even in its epigraphy.

Privately, without telling Mr Saltzmann, I took some of the Hebrew books from their place in the bookshelf, and worked through various passages that I found I could cope with. The easiest passages for me to read, all questions of grammar aside, were in the Bible, both because the stories I chose were already familiar to me, and because I could always check my understanding of what I'd read against the English version. One of the first of the tales I went through in this way, reading the Hebrew and English in alternation, was that in which God 'proved' Abraham by asking of him the sacrifice of 'his son, his only son, whom he loved, even Isaac,' before accepting the sacrifice of a ram caught in a thicket instead. 'And afterwards they rose up and went together to Beersheba; and Abraham dwelt in Beersheba.'

It was a curious experience to read it all in the original Hebrew for the first time, knowing that in Beersheba, which I had hoped to have visited by that time, there once again dwelt a Hebrew-speaking people who, like myself, were reputed to be descended from the tribe of Abraham and Isaac. How long, and in how many places, everything had been going on: fathers, sons, deaths, sheep, thornbushes, the lot.

4

'And Abraham expired and died in a good old age, an old man and full of years; and was gathered unto his people. And Isaac and Ishmael his sons buried him in the cave of Machpelah, in the field of Ephron . . .'

Well, it hadn't been quite like that. My father hadn't died. Modern medical science, personified by Dr Friedenberg and his colleagues, had seen to that. Nor was he all that old. He had in fact only just retired from work. Three months previously, seeing that none of his sons showed any interest in it, he had sold the cattlefeed plant he had established in the town many years before. Which, as everyone said, was a blessing, in view of what happened to him.

What happened to him, firstly, was that he woke one morning with a stomach ache. This wasn't altogether unusual; he was both choleric and dyspeptic by temperament. He dosed himself liberally with milk of magnesia, wandered about the house in dressing-gown and pyjamas, complaining to anyone who would listen to him about how rotten he was feeling, and then went to bed. Before driving into town that morning I went into his bedroom and asked if there was anything I could do for him. He answered with a peremptory 'No!' The curtains were drawn against the rays of the sun, but every corner of the room was irradiated with a faint yellow light that seemed more baffling to the eye than darkness itself. He had some kind of antiquated air-conditioning outfit in his room, a box-like affair the size of a small refrigerator, which rattled and wheezed and produced no cool air at all, so far as I could judge. The noise was distracting; his irritability was embarrassing; his illness was obviously not serious. I left him and went into town. My final exams at the university were a couple of weeks behind me, and my departure for Israel was booked for a few days ahead. I was a busy man, then; or felt myself to be one.

When I came back I found our family doctor in my father's room. There was a smell of disinfectant in the air. When I greeted my father there was no answer; he lay on his back with his head turned aside. I leaned over him and saw something glittering in the tiny hollow of bone next to his eye. His face contracted and he groaned; that bright spot shivered and disappeared. Only then did I realise it had been a tear.

The doctor had been putting his things into his case; he beckoned my mother and me to follow him out of the room. In the passage he said, 'I've given him something to ease the pain. He should settle down.' He added in a puzzled tone, 'It's the intensity of the pain that I don't like. If he isn't much better by tonight he'll have to go into hospital. For observation.'

The pain hadn't eased by evening; it had become far worse. His temperature had risen sharply; his groans rang through the house; he hardly knew where he was. He asked for water, for the doctor, for more blankets, for fewer blankets, for the air conditioner to be turned on, for it to be turned off. Under a grey bristle of beard his face was twisted into a new shape; his eyes shone with a light I had never seen in them before. The previous day he had been a trim, fit, firm-fleshed man just past middle-age, no more, vigorous in his movements, pugnacious in his expression, quick in his glances. And even in the morning he had appeared to be, at worst, an unwell, irritable old man indulging himself in a sense of grievance against the unreliability of his own body. But now, within a matter of hours, he had become a tormented stranger, other than himself, other to himself. What one saw in his eyes was not so much pain or fear as a stark incredulous glare of interrogation.

For what seemed minutes on end that glare would be fixed on one point or another in his room; then he would heave up in the bed, his lips uttering sounds, sighs, non-words; he would fall back into brief, uneasy snatches of sleep.

The doctor came again at sunset, and phoned immediately for an ambulance. When it came the patient was wheeled down the garden path on a stretcher, put in the back of the cumbersome vehicle and driven away. Some of our neighbours and the people across the road stood at their gates and watched the spectacle, enjoying to the utmost the solemnity and drama of it all.

Dr Friedenberg was artless, sincere, and conscientious. Born and bred in Lyndhurst, trained in Cape Town and Edinburgh, he was a stalwart, square-shouldered, flat-faced man, whose ears had suffered much damage as a result of his prowess during his medical student years, as a rugby lock-forward. When we stood together on the pavement his troubled face loomed many inches above mine in the dying light. He made no pretence at being omniscient. He confessed he was very puzzled. He said he was going to call in the town's one specialist physician immediately, for a consultation. Then they might have to call on the town's one specialist surgeon. Would I and my mother be at the hospital later that evening? I said I would be, and he walked away with his rolling rugby-player's stride to his car. I remember finding the purposefulness of that walk of his absurdly comforting.

My father was operated on early the next morning. At about eleven that night we were called to what proved to be the first of a series of vigils in anticipation of his death. Later he was operated on a second time, and a third; each operation being the result of a crisis, and each in turn producing other crises. There were vigils at midday, at night, in the dead hours of pre-dawn. The hospital was most punctilious in summoning us each time they believed him to be on the point of dying. But there was nothing we could do, once we were there, except sit about interminably in one waiting-room or another, or loiter up and down night-empty corridors, looking at the funereal vases of flowers that stood in front of every door.

When we were allowed into his room we witnessed deliriums, bouts of shuddering that looked violent enough to shake his joints apart, prolonged, sunken spells of nausea, when the expression on his unmoving, strangely averted features made one think his flesh had turned in disgust from itself. One night he choked and choked while the nurses spooned from his throat the mucus in which he appeared literally to be drowning. Apparatus of various kinds – stands, tubes, clamps, bottles of blood and saline fluid, oxygen cylinders of great weight in metal cradles – constantly stood or hung about his bed. You might have thought some sort of complicated industrial process was taking place, without which he could not die. A faint smell of suppuration came from his dressings. On his best days, when he wasn't totally unconscious or conscious only of pain and nausea, his hands wandered over the bedclothes, his lips constantly muttered meaningless words. The gaze of his eyes was sightless, turned inward; the interrogation that had been in them was quenched. His nose seemed to grow in length, but everything else about shrank from day to day, his arms in particular taking on an oddly slight, boyish, negligible appearance. The doctors and the nurses made no secret of their surprise that he was not dead.

He had never been so seriously ill before, and what had happened to him was as shockingly unexpected to us as if he had been the victim of some savage accident. Yet we also had to contend, day after day, then week after week, with the torment of slowness, doubt, and anticipation. During that time I came to think of his death as the true end of his life in a sense that had simply never occurred to me before: death was life's goal, its only certain aim and intention, it was the destination for the sake of which the journey was taken. It was not an unfortunate, retrograde flaw in nature's arrangements, an arbitrary, unnecessary interruption of life; it was not the last, most deplorable accident we would all have to endure. There was nothing arbitrary or accidental about it. My father's life had been a ceaseless, unknowing, unswerving trek towards these hideous days and hours; they were the summation of his life as well as its undoing. He had moved through time as through a landscape, distracted by a thousand moods, experiences, possessions, achievements, memories, but always, unfalteringly, in one direction only, in this direction. And as with him, so with everyone else who lived, or had ever lived, or ever would. So many deaths already! So many still to die!

Could any discoveries or revelations have been more commonplace? Indeed, no. That was just the point. That was precisely the thought which produced in me a kind of vertigo, associated in my mind with the long, darkly glistening, strictly regular corridors of the hospital. Afterwards, it was the only recollection I had of the stress within my body of shock, pity, or fear.

I had of course cancelled my flight to Israel; I couldn't leave in such circumstances. My departure had been put off indefinitely. I no longer gave it a thought. I could remember how eager I had been to leave home, to travel, to see new places, meet new people, and do new work. But I could no longer remember why I had wanted any of these things, I couldn't find my way back to wanting them.

5

It was then that I met Boaz, the Israelite. I found him on the farm. He came to the car as soon as I arrived one day, and asked if he could speak to me when I had finished what I had come to do.

The first thing you saw when you looked at Boaz was his blind eye. It was swollen, glaucous, without iris or pupil, always open. Its size and fixity were startling, even horrifying. What was more startling still, however, was your realization that while you had been staring at that dead, sightless orb, *he* had been regarding you, unobserved as it were, with his good eye. That one was small, yellow, lively, set under a wrinkled lid.

His head was shaven, his skin was drawn tight against the bones of his face, and lights shone in glints from its darkness. His body was painfully thin, melodramatically so, as if he had willed it to be like that in order to point some obscure yet incontrovertible moral. I wouldn't care to guess his age: he could have been anything between forty and sixty, perhaps more. His clothes were as ragged as those of any other farm African. When he walked it was with odd, stiff, elongated strides; when he stood still, he held himself with an almost soldierly uprightness.

His air of patience was indistinguishable, somehow, from confidence, as he waited near the car, not moving from it, while I went about my business. I had asked him to tell me at once what he wanted; but he had said no, he would rather wait to talk to me, it would be better. He wanted to talk to me alone – 'apart' was the word he used. Puzzled, curious, a little taken aback, I asked Piet, when we were a little distance from the car, who the stranger was; but all Piet would say was that his name was Boaz, that he had arrived on the farm a few days previously, and that he was some kind of preacher. He didn't know any more, Piet insisted, than that.

I'd arrived later than usual that afternoon, and I was more than usually conscientious about the sheep-counting. So by the time we were finished the sun was low in the west, red, growing larger; around it were gathering the clouds that invariably appeared in the western corner of the horizon at that hour, after even the most cloudless days. Those clouds, together with the dust that was always in the air, the flat openness of the country, and the strength of the sun, all combined to produce the most spectacular sunsets, day after day: immense, silent, rapid combustions that flared violently into colour and darkened simultaneously. It always seemed suddenly that you became aware that the colours had been consumed and that only the darkness remained; that the day was over, it would soon be full night.

My conversation with Boaz lasted longer than I had expected it to, though the request he actually had to make of me was simple enough. All he wanted, he said, speaking to me in Afrikaans, was my permission to live for a time on the farm, in one of the huts that neither Piet nor Kagisho used. (Altogether there were half-a-dozen small, mud-walled, iron-roofed huts for the African labourers, in a group sheltered by a screen of thornbushes some way behind the farm house.) He was an Israelite, Boaz told me. He was a preacher. He travelled about the country on foot, carrying his message to all who would listen. The destination of each of his journeys, he said, became known to him only after he had arrived at it. After each departure he knew that it had been right for him to move on again. Now he was here, having come from Lyndhurst along the Samarian Road; and here, it had been decided, was where he should stay.

An Israelite! Nothing less! Would he tell me who the Israelites were? He did so, at some length. Later I was to look up old newspaper files covering some of the events of which he had spoken. The facts he gave me were accurate enough. About half a century before, under the leadership of a certain Enoch Mgijima, one of the separatist African religious sects had rejected the New Testament as a white man's fiction and 'returned' to the worship of the one God of Israel. Inspired by its prophet the sect grew enormously in numbers and influence among the Africans in the bigger cities, until Mgijima called on his followers to gather at a village called Bulhoek, in order to celebrate the Passover. Several thousand obeyed him, coming together to feast and to pray for the coming of the Messiah. Days passed. Eventually the authorities told the people to move. They refused. One morning detachments of armed police arrived and ordered them to leave immediately. Instead of dispersing, the Israelites tried to attack the police who opened fire at close range. Hundreds were shot down. Those who survived fled or were arrested. Mgijima disappeared. Thereafter the movement went out of sight, was lost to any public record. However, some of the survivors of the Bulhoek massacre continued to meet as they had always done, in tiny, secret conventicles in the larger cities. It was from one of these that Boaz had come.

While he had been telling his story, we had left the car and walked a little way into the veld. Insects whirred out of the tussocks of grass at our feet; a single bird gave a melancholy, repeated whistle; I heard the voices of children from the huts, and in the distance the bleating of the sheep as they went down to graze. A faint evening breeze had sprung up. The blaze in the west was as fierce as it was remote.

His parents, Boaz went on, had been Israelites. They had taken him to their meetings, they had read the Bible to him every morning and evening, they had forbidden him to eat pork. But he had not been interested in their religion. He had wanted to be like all the other children who ran about in the streets and whose parents did not care what they did, or what they believed in, or what they ate. He left home as soon as he could, when he had been fourteen. He had had many jobs, of all kinds, in many places. He did not go home until years and years had passed. Then he heard one day that his father had died, and he decided he should go back, in order to comfort his mother.

During his first night at home he had a dream. He did not see God in his dream, for God could not be seen, but he heard Him. Everything was still and empty in the dream, and out of the stillness God spoke to him as if he were Joshua, saying 'The book of the law shall not depart out of thy mouth; but thou shalt meditate therein day and night that thou may do all that is written therein. Have I not commanded thee? Be strong and of a good courage; be not afraid neither be thou dismayed: for the Lord thy God is with thee whithersoever thou goest.' He woke, and knew that he had been chosen. He was a chosen man among those chosen people.

'Like I choose this stone,' Boaz said, stooping to pick up a faintly translucent pebble, and holding it out to me on the palm of his hand.

It was a kind that was common enough around Lyndhurst: irregular in shape, smooth to the touch, brown in colour, darkening inward from its shining surface, so that you could see some way into it, rather as with a lump of resin. I knew such stones to be volcanic in origin, like the diamonds that were mined in Lyndhurst. It lay in his hand, its dim light sealed eternally within it.

'Like this stone,' he went on calmly, not at all like a man putting forward a paradox, 'chooses me.'

He brought it closer to his good eye, bending his head over it. 'You think this stone is dead?' he asked me. 'You think it's here for nothing? No, never. It can't move, but it can wait for me, lying here, while all my life I've been coming nearer and nearer to it. You understand? Now I pick it up, and hold it, and look at it. See how it shines! Perhaps it speaks and sings also, only we can't hear it. But God can. Imagine! Imagine!' he repeated fervently, putting the stone to his ear. Then he held it to mine, his clenched hand against my temple.

I could hear only the blurred, small sounds of the evening breeze, nudging at intervals against me, on its journey across the empty country. I did not speak, but Boaz dropped his arm and looked down once more at the stone. With a jerk of his arm he flung it from him. We watched it fly through the air, a fast-moving, diminishing speck that fell out of sight, somewhere beyond the double-track that ran down from the farmhouse.

'So it's gone,' I said.

'Gone from us,' he corrected me. 'It's somewhere else now, where it has to be.'

A little later I asked him if he wanted to hold 'meetings' – I couldn't think of any other word to use – while he was on the farm. He was silent. I looked up into his gaunt, disfigured face. He blinded me with his blind eye. Then he said: 'I am holding a meeting now.'

I turned and began walking back to the car, parked forlornly on the rise. He followed me. I couldn't pretend myself that I had not been moved by his story. I had listened for the song he had said was locked in the stone; I envied his faith in the meaningfulness of his actions; I felt a bond with him in his absurd, wild claim that he, too, was some kind of Jew. Why shouldn't he be? What sort of Jew was I? Wasn't it possible that he knew more about the spirit and fervour of the Israelites than I ever would? That I might learn from him something that no one else could ever teach me? Yes, just because he was a poor, black, skeleton-thin zealot who had been 'sent' to live in a tumbledown hut on a farm that was nowhere. Just because he was a nut, a religious loony, a dreamer, a hearer of voices, a man you could do nothing with.

But all he had asked for me was permission to stay on the farm. It was easy for me to tell him that he could. 'But I don't want any trouble,' I said. 'Not with Piet, not with anyone. Do you understand?'

He held me in the disjunction of his stare or stares before assuring me that there would be no trouble.

6

During the first few weeks that followed, Boaz was as good as his word. When I went out to the farm Piet and Kagisho, who seemed proud to have Boaz living with them, told me that he spent a lot of time praying, and that he preached sometimes to them and to Africans from the neighbouring farms. On these visits Boaz himself invariably made a point of coming to see me, after I had finished with the others. He never asked me for food or money: presumably the others gave him the little he needed.

What he did ask for, however, during our early conversations, was information. Information about the Jews: he wanted to know what I could tell him about the Jewish dietary laws, about the festivals, about the liturgy, about the dispersion of the Jews to all the countries of the world, about Zionism and the State of Israel. Information about myself: he wanted to know who I was, what I was doing with myself, what I had done before he had met me, what I planned to do with my life. Information about current events, which he interpreted in ways I could not follow, according to various texts from the Bible. I answered all his questions as frankly as I could, and he listened carefully. We talked at the car, or in the car, or in the deserted house, or walking about the veld as we had the first time. He was always eager and exalted in his manner; but he was always polite and firm as well. Sometimes when he found himself at a loss for a word his lips would tremble, as if at the strain of containing the force momentarily pent up within him; but there was nothing swooning, babbling, hysterical, or ranting about him, even when he was at his most intense. He was utterly humourless, and utterly direct. He made less of the difference in colour between us – and the difference it meant in status, legal rights, opportunities, wealth, education – than any other African I had ever met. That he believed in an omnipresent God and I did not was the only difference between us that mattered at all in his eyes. Or eye, rather.

It was after we had had three or four such conversations that Boaz unexpectedly told me one day that he now knew why he had been 'sent' to the farm. It was his task to convert me to a belief in God. He had been 'chosen' to do so.

'Oh no!' I remember exclaiming absurdly, as if he had just broken an item of bad news to me.

'Yes, I will do it with God's help,' he answered. 'You will rejoice when it has been done.'

We were standing where we had stood several times before, on the rise near the car; the sunset was once again blazing away on our right. But in the week that had passed since I had last seen him there had been a brief, fierce, dust-laden blast of wind from the direction where the sun was setting; and it was now much cooler than it had been, winter was beginning. Boaz had buttoned his threadbare jacket and turned up the lapels. He waited for my response. I could see that he, at any rate, was already rejoicing in what he was to accomplish.

'No,' I said again. 'No, Boaz. You must leave me alone.'

'How can I?' he asked. 'You are not alone. You never have been.'

He was immovable, utterly dedicated to the task he believed he had been set; as single-minded as I was fragmented in my emotions. I was acutely embarrassed. I was touched and flattered that the welfare of my soul should mean so much to him. I was ashamed to think that secretly, without ever admitting to myself what I was really doing, I had invited him to make such an attempt for me, or on me. I was sorry I had encouraged him by talking to him as much as I had. I was resentful that he should feel free to tamper with my beliefs, or lack of belief. I was afraid that he might succeed.

The next time I went out to the farm Piet said to me, with a curious, sideways, lingering glance quite unlike any I had previously had from him, that Boaz was 'always praying for the baas'.

When we returned from the *kraal* I could see Boaz waiting for me near the car, as he always did. What was I to do? To avoid him altogether? To try to talk him out of his mission? To humour him, to pretend that he had succeeded, in the hope that he would leave me alone, leave the farm, believing his duty done? Should I simply tell him to go, to get out, that the permission I'd given him to stay on the farm was withdrawn? Or should I say to him that he would never, never get me to recognize his God, no matter how passionately he prayed for me, or tried to get me to pray with him? That even if there was a God I was by nature deaf to him, blind to him, insensible to his touch on me?

In the end I tried all these ways of dealing with Boaz, as well as another that took me profoundly by surprise, and with which I persisted far longer than I had with any of the others. I tried to believe, as Boaz wanted me to, in a God of life and death, the God my ancestors had believed in through their thousands of years of history; a God who was present in Lyndhurst or on the farm; who cared whether my father recovered from his illness or did not, and who had his reasons for prolonging his life or ending it, as he had with the lives of all other men; a God who would sustain me in my own life, and in the knowledge of whom I would find the purpose and the sense of ultimate value I needed. I tried to pray, I tried to read as much of the Bible as I could in Hebrew and English, I went to the synagogue on Friday evenings and Saturday mornings, I tried *faute de mieux* to pretend or imagine that I did already believe, in the hope that the genuine belief would follow.

Boaz was not the only one who helped me during this

period of trial. Though I did not tell Mr Saltzmann about Boaz, or about what he was trying to do for me, or about what I was trying to do for myself, I had consulted Mr Saltzmann about some of the points of Jewish ritual Boaz had raised, he had noticed my attendance at the synagogue, and he must have found my mood or attitude more sympathetic to his faith than it had previously been. At any rate, our lessons were soon being neglected more shamefully than ever before; and Mr Saltzmann revealed a kind of ironic ardour that he had previously hidden from me. He swayed in his chair, he blew his nose, he made his points in the air with an extended, startled forefinger; he tipped his hat forward with a flick from behind, so that its brim was low over his forehead, and thrust it back to run his fingers through his hair; he spoke of Jerusalem and Babylon and the Vilna Gaon, of Auschwitz, of Isaiah, and the Baal Shem Tov. If Boaz spoke most often of God's power, seeing it figured forth as much in the decisions and acts of every day as in the pageant of nature's cruder, simpler effects that was constantly displayed between our bald stretch of earth and the sky above, Mr Saltzmann talked more of God's justice and mercy. He spoke of how unthinkable it was that everything men and women had always had to endure should go unrecorded, unnoticed, unrecompensed, for age after age, empire after empire, life after life; of how inconceivable it was that his, Mr Saltzmann's, demand for justice had no connexion with the innermost workings of history, with the intentions of the universe, with the final nature of reality.

In his way Mr Saltzmann, too, was impressive. But I admit his words had less effect on me, when I was in his presence, than those of Boaz: partly because Mr Saltzmann was so much more familiar to me, and so much less fanatical, but mostly because it was Boaz who, after all, had declared my conversion to be his mission. 'Why *me*?' I asked him, more than once, in remonstrance, or anger, or amusement; and he invariably answered me, as he had before, with all passion and sincerity, 'We have been chosen to choose each other. We belong to the people of Israel.' I could not get beyond that conviction, beneath it, over it. 'Is he still praying for me?' I asked Piet once or twice, and he answered me with an air of unsmiling rebuke, 'Always'.

So I went back and forth between Mr Saltzmann in Lyndhurst and Boaz on the farm; often I went out to the farm when I had no business there other than to see Boaz. I made no attempt to bring the two believers together. I felt, almost superstitiously, that I could do so only if I had brought them together within myself; only if through them I had arrived at a comprehension that would make my acquaintance with them both, at that particular time in my life, self-justifying, self-explanatory, reasonable, an illustration of the necessary principles of our shared existence. I argued with them both, I challenged them both, I denounced them both. There were times when I told myself that I was doing no more than studying them as specimens, or that I was practising some kind of hoax on them, or that I was kindly doing them a favour in pretending to be interested in their preposterous beliefs. Yet even when I said such things to myself I remained convinced that if I ever let shame, guilt, embarrassment, or my own critical mind inhibit me from what I was doing, I would always regret it, I would always believe that I had let slip an extraordinary chance which would never recur.

Invariably, every day, I still called in at the hospital. To the astonishment of the doctors my father had plainly begun to recover; Dr Friedenberg had finally summoned up the courage to say, 'I think we'll soon be able to say that he's out of danger.' In all, four months were to pass before he emerged from the hospital.

7

The farm had always been far more of a hobby or extravagance of my father's than a source of income; he was what his Afrikaner neighbours called a *tjek-boek boer*, a checkbook farmer. At different times he had put a great acreage under the plough and planted mealies; he had gone in for the breeding of karakul lambs; he had attempted to raise pedigree Red Poll cattle. None of these enthusiasms had turned out well. The mealies died of drought; he lost his appetite for karakul breeding when he found that the lambs had to be slaughtered at the age of three days if their pelts were to realize the highest value; the pedigree bull he had bought lacked the progenitive urge. It was fortunate for me that nothing more complicated than speculation in sheep was the current activity on the farm; the animals were simply supposed to graze on the veld until such time as they were sent to the sales in Lyndhurst.

I was surprised, therefore, that when he began to make his first attempts to come out of the utter seclusion and isolation of his illness, my father should have asked me as often as he did about the farm. His business having been sold, I suppose he felt the farm to be the only hold he now had on the world of possessions, of activity, of competition, of buying and selling at known prices, in which he had lived for so long and from which he had been so abruptly sundered. Usually when I went to see him he still lay silent on the bed, with an expression on his face that was remote, abstracted, almost aristocratic in its detachment and insubstantiality. But if he did no more than greet me with a flicker of his eyelids or a few indifferent words, almost invariably he would later ask me if I had been out to the farm, if I had found everything there in order, if it had rained on the farm, if I thought Piet was carrying out his job properly. Because I could see it pleased him if I said I had just been out there, or was on the point of going out, I said these things even when they weren't true.

However, one day when he asked me what was happening on the farm, I began to tell him about Boaz. Previously I hadn't mentioned to him that Boaz was living there. But now I described how I had found him on the farm, and how he had spoken to me, and what he looked like; I repeated what I had learned from him about the Israelite sect, and about his own life. I tried also to say something about the nature of Boaz's belief in God: how absolute it was, and how direct; how he saw God's purposes plainly written everywhere; how he believed himself to have been chosen by God and yet at liberty to deny his chosenness, in a world in which everything was foreknown yet undetermined. The one subject about which I said nothing was the plan that Boaz had for me, and my own reactions to it. I felt I shouldn't speak of that until I knew, in the simplest way, where I stood. Then I would either need to say everything about it, or never speak of it at all.

But my voice and manner must have shown my father that Boaz had become much more to me than a freak about whom I could tell amusing anecdotes. At any rate, early in my story I noticed that the sick man was listening to me with a curious intentness; but it wasn't until I'd almost finished that I realized just how strangely he was looking at me, and in what a disturbed, random way he was moving his hands about on the bedclothes. At once I felt that I had been inconsiderate; in my preoccupation with Boaz I had gone on for much too long and overtired him. So I brought the story to an end as quickly as I could. 'I hope he'll still be around when you get up,' I said. 'Then you'll be able to see him for yourself.'

'No! I don't want to see him!' he exclaimed, with an inexplicable, weak urgency in his voice. 'You must tell him to go. You mustn't wait. You must chase him away.'

'Why?' I asked in surprise.

He tried to sit up, but managed to do no more than get his head a few inches from the pillows before it fell back. Then he said again, 'Tell him he must go.'

'But why?' I insisted. 'What's the matter? He's doing no harm to anyone. He isn't making any trouble. He's just – just – '

'Tell him he must go.'

I couldn't argue with him about it; he was too weak. 'All right,' I said.

But I had no intention of doing what he'd told me. For Boaz's sake I couldn't do it; for my own; even in a way for my father's. I felt that the demand had come out of the weakness and disorder of his illness, it was nothing more than a sick man's whim.

The next time I went to see him I thought he might well have forgotten the whole conversation. But I'd hardly come into the room before he asked me, as if he'd been thinking of nothing else since we had last spoken. 'Have you been to the farm? Have you told that man to go?'

'Yes,' I said. 'I told him. He'll be going soon. You don't have to worry about it.'

'Soon isn't good enough. He must go at once. I don't want him there. I don't want him on my place.'

'But why not?' I protested. 'What have you got against him?'

Again I didn't get a direct reply. After some minutes, however, he began to ramble in a disconnected yet obsessive way about Boaz – or rather, about 'that man, who calls himself an Israelite'. His voice was so low that I had to strain to hear him; his words were interspersed with the louder sounds of his breathing, or with spells when he merely moved his lips without producing any sounds. The incoherent craziness of what he was saying was made more painful by the physical effort that went into it, and by the earnestness with which he searched my face in every silence for my reaction to his words.

That man who called himself an Israelite, he said, was responsible for his illness. He was a usurper, an enemy, a demon, an evil spirit. He wanted him to die. He came to take what wasn't his. He had to be driven away. At once. Couldn't I have seen it? How could I have let him stay there for so long? What had I thought I was doing? Hadn't I understood that it was a matter of life and death? Yes, life and death, nothing less. That man was a *malakh ha-movess*, an angel of death. He was waiting to finish his work, he would stay there as long as he was allowed to. But I could drive him away if I really wanted to. Unless I was in league with him and was also waiting for him to finish what he had come to do . . .

So he went on, interminably. It was pathetic, tedious, unnerving. His eyes, filled with fear and reproach, would not leave me. I tried to soothe and reassure him; but when he finally fell silent it was not, I felt, because I had succeeded but simply because he was too fatigued to go on. He beckoned me to come closer, and grasped my hand; his touch was hot and dry. 'You must also take care,' he said in a voice laden with anxiety and foreboding. 'You mustn't think it'll be different for you. You understand? You won't escape either. When he's finished with me then it'll be your turn. I'm worried for you also – '

'Don't worry,' I interrupted him. 'I understand. You must rest now. Everything will be all right. I'll do what you want me to do.'

He lay on his back, his nose raised towards the ceiling, his mouth pinched beneath it. His hands were on his breast, rising and falling with every breath he took. I sat by the side of the bed until he had sunk into a doze. He did not stir when I crept out of the room.

Outside the hospital the afternoon air was tepid, still, yellow. Shadows stretched over dusty lawns and dejected beds of flowers. In the road beyond the hospital grounds was a war memorial: an incised concrete slab, surrounded by steps, chains, cast-iron rifles stacked in threes. The unreality of my father's words infected everything around me, everything I thought of. Yet I felt that I was seeing them again for what they were, after too long a lapse. Streets and buildings were nothing more than forms of a common inertness; my thoughts nothing more than forms of delusion. What kind of imbecile, self-indulgent credulity or conceit had been keeping me going between Boaz and Mr Saltzmann these last few weeks? In what way were my superstitious hopes or expectations better founded than my father's wild fears? He at least had the excuse of having been weakened almost to the point of death by his illness; whereas I had done no more than watch his struggles.

Because my car was parked facing towards town, away from home, I drove in that direction. It was a Saturday afternoon; the shops were closed and the streets were more than usually empty. No one was about in the Market Square, except for a group of youths sitting on their motor bikes, gunning their engines and shouting at one another, going nowhere. I turned to the right: more closed shops, a bridge over some railway lines. A little further on was the fence around an abandoned mine, and then streets of low, iron-roofed houses. A few more minutes, a few more turns, and they were behind me. The town was behind me, though the mine-dumps still straggled alongside the road for some distance. I came to the crossing from which the Samarian Road ran off to one side, and I left the main road to join it. It seemed that I was going to the farm.

Why not? Once more I went along the dreary, winding, familiar route. If town had been emptier than usual, the road was busier. Several family parties had chosen to go along it for their Saturday afternoon outings. Now their cars were parked at various unremarkable spots along the road. The adults sat just outside the cars, listening on portable radios to commentaries on the big rugby matches; the children ran about in the veld, jumping on or off the antheaps, or playing hide-and-seek in the scrub.

By the time I reached the farm I'd left behind the last of these groups. Once through the cattle-grid, the road ran straight for a mile or so, then swerved a little to begin the short ascent to the farmhouse and the *koppies* behind. From a distance the house looked no more substantial than a box, with the lines of the *kraals* and outbuildings scratched around it. The huts where Piet and the others lived were out of sight, hidden behind their shelter of thornbushes.

I pulled up the car in front of the house. No one came to greet me. I didn't expect anyone to come. I hadn't said that I would be paying a visit to the farm that day, so even if the car had been seen approaching along the road, it would have been taken to be someone merely passing through on his way to Platkop or the farms beyond. I sat in the car for a little while, listening to the ticking noises made by the engine as it cooled. Nothing moved about me. I could hear no other sound. Eventually I opened the door and stepped outside.

It was only when I was crossing the bare space between the house and the grove of thornbushes some distance behind it that I realized why I was there. I had come to tell Boaz that he had failed. He was welcome to stay on the farm or to leave it, as he wished. But I no longer had anything to say to him or any interest in listening to what he had to say to me.

8

The ground between the thornbushes had been turned into soft sand by the coming and going of the people who lived there. So my footsteps made no sound as I approached. The first that was known of my presence was when one of the yellow, long-tailed dogs which were always hanging around the place got to its feet and ran forward, barking loudly. By then I had already come upon the congregation gathered in front of the hut which Boaz had taken for himself.

About a dozen people were there, apart from Piet and Kagisho and their families. I knew none of the other drab, raggedly dressed, undersized men and women, farm labourers and their wives, who were squatting on the ground. In front of them stood Piet, with a Bible in one hand and in the other a long stick or stave surmounted by a Star of David plaited out of twigs. Next to him, on an iron bedstead, his body covered by a confusion of dirty blankets, lay Boaz. The sight of the bed dragged out into the open air, exposed to the sunlight, was somehow in itself almost as shocking or unnatural as Boaz's look of illness, collapse, abandonment, even decay.

He looked very ill indeed, like a dying man. His face was grey in colour, small, annulled, lightless. His lips were parted, his eyes closed. He was totally unconscious; the only person there who was unaware that I had come. The others had turned to look at me resentfully, as an intruder, a spy, a white enemy; and hopelessly, too, as someone who had the power to stop what they were doing and send them packing, and would probably do so. Only the children, the oval whites of their eyes immense with expectation and pent-up excitement, seemed pleased by the distraction my arrival offered.

No one moved or spoke. The sun shone down from a great height on the sand, huddled people, huts of mud and scraps of iron, the unconscious man on the bed. Heavy shadows merged indistinguishably on the sand. The dogs sniffed cautiously at my feet and wagged their curving tails. In the silence a sheep bleated loudly, resonantly, with a kind of ferocity of protest contained in the very helplessness and tremulousness of the sound. Until then I hadn't noticed the creature, tethered by a piece of rope around its neck to a thorntree a few yards away, on one side. It jerked its head, opened its mouth, and again the noise exploded, an astonishingly loud call or yell to come from such a small cavern of flesh and bone. High, full, vibrating, the noise went on for longer than seemed possible, maddening in its stridency and urgency, in its stupidity and comprehension alike. Even while the noise still rang in my ears, I found myself looking at Piet and he at me: in the look we exchanged I knew, among some other more surprising and important facts, that that clamorous sheep was not his.

I can't say for how long we stared at one another. He was bareheaded; and the unfamiliar prominence of his hard, round, shaven skull made him look like a stranger. He took a deep breath, as if to meet a challenge, raised his stave in the air, and began to speak in a tone I had never heard from him before. He was no longer the businessman *manqué* that I had known, or the patient, slyly submissive underling, or the conscientious shepherd. Or if he was still a shepherd, it was quite another flock, which he was leading to pastures I had never seen. His voice was loud, hectoring, defiant, his gestures were bold and emphatic. He had won back the attention of his audience immediately. One or two of them still glanced anxiously at me from time to time, but even they, like the others, were answering Piet's cries and exhortations with cries of their own, or with murmurs that they took up in turn from one another, or with phrases that they chanted in unison until Piet silenced them with a single wave of his hand. The little congregation swayed and moaned, the people clutched at the dust with their hands or clapped them together, they sat still and tense when Piet lowered his voice to a whisper. Whenever he turned to the recumbent, motionless figure of the sick man on the bed, opening his arms wide or lifting them high into the air as he did so, his audience was utterly silent, as if waiting for the sick man himself to rise and answer the speech breaking continually above him.

I couldn't understand a word of what Piet was saying.

Not a word. He was speaking one of the African languages: a speech that to my ears was composed entirely of clicks, trills, gutturals, deep plosives. Completely cut off from his meanings, I couldn't even tell where one word ended and another began. Yet, as in a dream, I felt that the incomprehensible sounds he was uttering were directed more specifically to me than to anyone else in his audience. The others may have forgotten about me; but I was certain that Piet had not.

As in a dream, too, foreknowledge and knowledge after the event were commingled inextricably in my mind. Each event surprised me as it took place; but once it had happened it seemed to me that it was just what I had been waiting for ever since I had come. Yes, Piet would abruptly bring his speech to an end, at a moment when no one had apparently expected him to do so. Yes, he would point at two men in the congregation, who would get hastily to their feet and go to the tethered sheep. Yes, one of them would grab it by the ears from behind and pull it back, making it rear up momentarily, before the other man knocked its hind legs off the ground. It sat grotesquely upright on its rump, with its forelegs dangling forward, its head pulled back, its throat exposed. Yes, inevitably, Piet would cross the space between himself and the pair struggling with the sheep; he would take a clasp knife from his pocket and open it; he would bring it to the animal's throat, and then, with a deft sweep, do no more than sever the rope.

The maddened animal plunged, screamed, kicked, collapsed, was dragged upright again. Once more it sat in an artificial man-like posture, its thin forelegs held up in front of it with a curiously finicking helplessness, a disgusting daintiness. It showed its even teeth, its tongue, its wide, flat nostrils. Its eyes were rolled back into its dark head. It looked like a shrunken, demented old man; the men kneeling or stooped around it, their faces clenched with absorption, were animalized, rapt, barely conscious.

And now?

Yes, of course, once he had done it I had known all along that he would. Piet pointed at me, with the hand in which he held the knife, and at last spoke in a language I could understand.

'You can see how sick Boaz is. This morning he fell, and since then he has not been able to get up. His heart is failing him. So we ask God to take this sacrifice, instead, and to let our teacher live.'

Then he raised his voice, his hand still outstretched. 'Boaz has prayed for you, many days. Now you will pray for him.'

He held out the knife to me. The lamb plunged. I came towards it. Its eye was a yellow blaze of life, crossed by a black, expressionless, oblong pupil.

9

Boaz died the next morning, in the African section of the Lyndhurst General Hospital, to which I had brought him in the car. Piet had been right in his diagnosis. He had succumbed, Dr Friedenberg said, to a 'massive coronary occlusion'. So the sacrifice was in vain.

Yes, I did do what had been asked of me. Under the blade of the knife I felt something soft and thick, then a resilience which suddenly failed, and the knife entered a hollow place behind it, a vacancy. It was a squalid, messy, pointless, godless act. Even while I was doing it I remembered as a child cutting open a tennis ball to see what was inside: the sensations under my hand were much the same. But the cutting of the sheep's throat was followed by a heavy spout of blood, and by cries of exultation from the others that were indistinguishable from cries of grief. It was followed, too, by a sudden fit of rage within me that made me lash out with the blade again, even though it could do no more than it had already done. I wanted to punish the sheep for dying under my hand; I wanted to revenge myself against Boaz against my father, for compelling me to be there and to learn what I had from them.

The outburst left me feeling calmer, a little tired, anxious to help Boaz in whatever way I could. The others made no objections when I said I would take him with me to hospital in Lyndhurst. Driving back to town, with Boaz awkwardly bundled into the back seat, I remember how consoling I found the emptiness of the countryside around me, its width, its indifference, its hard materiality. It was there, it would last. That was something to be grateful for, I felt then, not resentful of, as I had always been in the past.

I left Lyndhurst for Israel a few weeks later, carrying with me Mr Saltzmann's parting gift of a *siddur*, containing the daily prayers of the Hebrew liturgy. My father had come home just before I left, though he was still confined to his bed for a month or so. During that time he arranged for a white foreman, a Boer by the name of Klaas Eybers, to live on the farm and work it with him, on a profit-sharing basis.

My father never again mentioned Boaz to me, and I did

not speak of him either. Some years afterwards I learned that Piet had left the farm just after my own departure. He had gone, my father said, into 'the religion business' in one of the African townships around Lyndhurst, and had made a very good thing out of it. He had established his own church. My father had no idea what kind of rites were followed in it, but he did know that the money Piet got from his followers he invested in his ever-growing flock of sheep. He paid a fixed sum per head to continue grazing them on the farm.

Maggie Ross

Death by Drowning

I have been waiting here with you for a long time now. You will remember that I waited here. You will vouch that I worried about my wife.

What time do you close this place in the winter? It can't be much fun here after dark, with the wind hitting these thin walls, and only the sound of the sea on the stones below. If I was you, and in this hut, I would fear the wind in the winter. I would think, as I felt it rushing down this pier, that I too would be swept into the sea with the bits of rope, and torn canvas, broken signs, and ancient paper. There are wooden seats at the end of the pier which someone has tied to the rails. You tied them? How wise, to know the strength of winds. I expect you did it when the blizzards first began and the snow came. What was it like on this pier in the snow? Did the wind sweep it in great piles against the pavilions? I can imagine it, white, with the sea below, in green slabs, frozen. Were there any seagulls about then? Any boats able to tie up at the end of the pier?

I've been waiting for my wife for a long time now. I am very worried. You can see that. She can't be down there still, can she? Surely there is no one left down there at the end, on this sort of day. Everyone who passes your window moves so fast with their faces held down that I might have missed her, while in here with you. The chances are that I have missed her, but I'll wait for the sky to clear; it sometimes does in the early spring. Look at all those people staggering past, worn out with the wind. With winter hardly over, out they come like gnats, trying to hover in a patch of sun. But the wind disperses them and gives them a buffeting. Look at them in their great-coats, holding on to their collars, attempting to enjoy their ridiculous Sunday perambulation. It wasn't my idea to come today. The idea was Miriam's. All winter she has nagged at me to take the Sunday walk. As if I was in control of the weather. Today she said, 'Spring's coming. Must get down the pier again.' And now she's missing.

I'm not a man for the wind-swept sea-scape, but to Miriam it is life itself. For ten years now she has seen the sea at least once a week: with me to hang on to, and me to wait while she indulged her passion for salt air. She has always leaned on me. She's fond of the open: this pier is a regular haunt of hers. Walk down, ride back on the train; or sometimes walk both ways if she felt impatient. She made me wait for her out there, by that glass wall. When I gave up going with her all the way I used to wait by the glass wall in an effort to keep out of the wind. But there are gaps in the wall and the wind cuts right through you, like a knife. I used to walk up and down sometimes, to keep warm; sometimes as far as the kiosk where the girl used to serve ice-cream. Do you remember last year's ice-cream girl? I ate ice-cream to keep the salt taste from my lips. I find salt sickening. Don't you? No. I don't suppose you do, this is your life and you like the salty air. So does Miriam.

Listen to the wind now. It's in the East: it must be at gale force. Look at the way it lifts the lino by the door, and swings the light. Aren't you afraid for the windows? That they might crack inward with the force? Or perhaps this wind is not so strong as I might think. You know more about these things than I. You are the authority.

At the end of the pier, on the sun deck, there is a café whose windows have been shuttered. The shutters are made of plastic stretched on wooden frames. You made them? They are needed down there where the wind is in full force.

You would know the force of the wind, and have it on a chart somewhere in here. There must be nothing about wind that you don't know; its velocity and strength. Could it, for instance, blow a person overboard? A fairly small person? Is it possible on a day like this, do you think? Could it blow a person into the sea? Up on the sun deck at the end of the pier I saw a woman's hat fly over the side as she tried to snatch it from the air. I saw her twist and fall against the rails. And she was quite a big lady. The wind is strong. I'm sure that it can blow people into the sea. Small people of course.

Miriam is frail; her word not mine. She says she's frail. In winter clothing she weighs seven stone four. That isn't heavy. She has ill-health, but it doesn't do to under-estimate her strength. She eats a lot. She requires attention, and help in the house for the many duties to be performed. I do not know the nature of her illness except that it requires a diet and fresh air: both self-imposed of course. A little bit depressing, the sick, don't you think? They tend to make impossible demands. Complaints are made; feelings registered: there is a great loss of freedom with the sick. Their requirements are excessive, their consideration nil.

Miriam should be here by now.

You can see how thoughtless she is to make me wait like this. It has always been the same. She has always left me waiting in the cold. I suffer from the cold, but Miriam never does. She cannot understand about my feeling cold. Her blood is permanently hot. There is a dog from Mexico with blood like that. It has hot blood and not a single hair. Neither has Miriam. She has no hair – except on her head, of course. She has none under her arms or on her legs, and none on her face, or anywhere at all. Some women have a lot of hair, and attractive little moustaches: there's not a hair on Miriam to cover that thick skin of hers. Her skin is like an elephant's: thick and old. She doesn't feel the cold, and never wears a hat. Do you suffer from ear-ache?

I have had ear-ache now for ten years. My ears can't stand

the cold, or draughts. Miriam opens windows; she opens them in the house and she opens them in the shed. She would open them in my greenhouse too, if I wasn't there to watch her. Miriam could be called a Fresh Air Fiend. People like that need watching; they are dangerous. It is no joke to open all the greenhouse windows when the snow is on the ground. Much damage is done to delicate plants that require constant heat. Do you know anything about Orchids?

Getting dark quickly isn't it? Look at that cloud up there. Been like it ever since we got here. That cloud is raining. Can you see the grey streaks underneath? It was just like that when we arrived. The tide was not out then, but the sky was full of grey. We caught the train.

We caught the train to take us down the pier. We sat listening to the rhythmic sound of carriages on rails, looking out to sea through windows flecked with rain, and watched the receding shore change from white to grey, under trailing clouds. The rain increased, and at the other end we ran again for shelter, to the Lifeboat station. While sheltering there we made our five-hundredth inspection of the Lifeboat. I noted once again the devices for saving life, on show as though the place was a museum. Everything looked quite immovable: the Lifeboat anchored by a chain which held it firmly into place above the ramp, down which it is supposed to slide; the seaward doors firmly closed. And all the yellow oilskins hanging from the ceiling in rows, like giant flowers. On the way back I looked again into the Lifeboat station, but Miriam wasn't there.

She wasn't there.

Do you know anything about Orchids? I grow them. Orchids are my speciality, in fact my *life*. They are difficult to nurture it's true, but well worth the effort and the price. I bought a beauty from the Horticultural Show. I beat a Maharajah to the price; it cost me five whole pounds. He wanted it, but so did I. I always get what I want, eventually. The spray of bloom was two feet long. You should have seen it when it came: each bloom packed in its own plastic cup, and the plant wrapped in Sphagnum Moss. I nursed it well, and now it's showing newer growth, my Odontoglossum. Orchids are not exactly temperamental, but you learn to know your plants. I feed them water in which bones have been soaked, and spray the greenhouse twice a day. They like the hot, damp air, and so do I. We get on well together. In my greenhouse I can breathe: it seems the only place where I can. Do you understand? No? You're not alone. Miriam cannot understand me either. She treats flowers as her enemies. Today she's in her element, getting her fill of salt. What time did you say you closed this place?

Perhaps I should have gone straight home instead of reporting this affair to you. Perhaps when I get home Miriam will be there. She likes to play a joke on me. She has played jokes on me before, like when she used to leave me standing in the cold. At Christmas time she played a joke. She said at first it was a burglar's work, and *he* had put them back. But I knew that she had done it; every plant had been returned into its rightful place, even the Laelias which hung from the roof. There was a lot of damage done; blossoms broken off, leaves snapped. No burglar would have brought them back, like she did, with destruction everywhere and the door left open for the wind to penetrate. That was Miriam's joke. She tends to get playful at festival time. She said it was the only way that she could think of, to get me indoors for Christmas. She was being playful you see. All day I thought my flowers were gone, but she appeared at dinner with three blooms on her dress: perfect specimens of my Cymbidium Scorpio. I wished then that they had had a sting. Orchids are very fragile and need a lot of care. Women are tough compared with them. It takes a lot to get rid of a woman. Where did I last see my wife? I told you.

We were up on the sun deck and standing by the Ladies. She said she wanted to go in there, and that I must wait for her. I stood by the weighing-machine until the rain began to fall, then wandered under cover where they keep the Fun

Fair. It was very dark in there, the stalls all covered up; pieces of canvas and rotting scenery about the place. I opened a door marked 'Aquarium, This Way': there was nothing inside. Miriam may have passed by while I was in there. She suffers from short sight. She tends to lose things easily, and may have missed me in the dark. None of the machines was working, except the Speak-Your-Weight. I have a theory she may have wandered out of there and walked around outside. Perhaps she even went below, to look more closely at the sea. Did I tell you she was myopic?

The sea is a nasty shade of green today, not quite khaki, not quite brown. It has the look of camouflage. At the end of the pier the sea changes colour as it clears the last of the stanchions. The current is strong there, is it not? It looked as though it was swirling there, in circles or eddies: you would know more of these nautical terms than I. Is it very deep there, at the end of the pier? Now, I mean, now that the tide is out. No, not now, perhaps a little earlier before the tide turned. Now there are patches of mud and shell, which weren't there when we took the train. They weren't even visible below the water before the tide turned. In this weather the water is opaque; nothing can be seen under it, not even near the surface can things be seen, even floating things. The water is rendered opaque by mud which is churned up from the bottom. At the end of the pier the water is muddy. Why, if the water is deep? And it's *very* deep there, isn't it? Forgive my curiosity, but I am most interested in the construction of this pier. What a feat of engineering. How many years it must have taken for men to drive those piles into the mud: always with the shifting tides and the dreadful sight of the khaki sea below. It must have been terrible to look down. A feat of engineering for the sake of stupid people who take walks on a Sunday. Not content with mere walks they had to be entertained as well, with puppet shows, and Speak-Your-Weight machines, and Push-the-Skittles-Over.

I am worried about my wife, and to you I can speak

freely. I fear that she may have drowned. If the water is deep at the end of the pier, then she may have fallen in. Did I tell you that Miriam is short-sighted? She is short-sighted and I suffer from vertigo. How long were we on the end of the pier? I can't remember now.

I know that after the rain had stopped we left the Lifeboat station. We wandered along the wet boards and stopped to look for the speedboat. It is sometimes out at this time of year, but it wasn't in sight anywhere. There were no boats to be seen, except along the shore where they lay stranded facing the land. We walked along the promenade and up the wide steps to the sun deck. The café was closed, the canvas chairs stacked in rows against its doors. The canvas steamed when the sun came out. But there was no shelter up there from the dreadful wind which seemed to whip into every corner. I tried to shelter, but Miriam made me walk. She said it would do me good. She leaned over the rails to watch the tide. I saw a woman's hat fly off. We stayed on the upper deck, walking round and round, peering into deserted buildings. We saw the speedboat in a shed. Last year's paint was chipping off. They will launch it when the weather improves. No one would risk it on a day like this. Even the stairs are impossible to use – by the look of them. We didn't go below. We could hear the sea slapping but never went to look because I suffer from vertigo. All we did was the same as everyone: we wandered round and round, in and out, through the light and shade. Then Miriam went to the Ladies. That was the last time I saw her. I went into the Fun Fair. It was dark in there. She may have missed me. Or perhaps it was another of her jokes: her leaving me to wait. She might have gone below to see the sea; descending those slippery steps and walking down there among the barnacles and seaweed. The wind is very strong today. She could easily have fallen in.

But there must have been fishermen down there by the water. People fish all the year round. I may have seen some boys fishing from the steps where the speedboat ties up in the summer. There is no reason to suppose that boys wouldn't fish down there under the sun deck. Boys don't mind smells, or the whine of the wind. They don't have so far to cast their lines, and it's quiet down there for the throw. People passing overhead make only the faintest stamping with their feet. The boards are so thick, so far above, all sound is dulled. There is no noise but the wind, and the water, slapping the stanchions. Down there, if you look where it is dark, a pattern emerges: cross-stays and verticals. They show up white against the khaki sea because they are encrusted with barnacles. They resemble stars. They strain the wind through their members when it blows from the East. Do you know what it reminds me of down there under the pier? A slaughterhouse. That is why I never go down there now. I never go down, like I used to. It reminds me of a slaughterhouse, with the bare boards stretching away in straight lines. Nothing but wood and iron. There are chains down there to prevent you falling. They swing in the wind. There are iron hooks black with tar. The pillars down there are so thick they can hide a person standing behind one of them. I used to hate it down there when Miriam made me go. 'Down to the Slaughterhouse,' she would say, 'or a ride in the speedboat. Which?'

People shouldn't be allowed down there on a day like this, with the wind at force and coming from the East. Who knows, there might be an accident, a boy blown overboard: a chain is not enough to hold a boy who is casting a line in such a wind. You can't keep a hold on the boards with your feet. Learn which way the wind blows, that's the secret, then stand with your back to it – but be careful to hold on an iron pillar when you stand near the edge. Do your throwing quickly – there she goes. But throw it into the wind and you get it back in your face. Coming back across slippery boards is a nasty sensation, there are the steps to climb. Nasty sensation, looking up when crossing the gaps: 'Head up now. We are nearly there. If you funk it I'll make you ride in the speedboat too.' The coming back is bad: you are alone and you see the steps in front looking wider than before, and the sea showing through, swirling below you in khaki circles, making a sucking sound. You slip on the steps as you reach the top. The eyes aren't used to the change of light and the sudden enormity of the sky. My eyes panicked at the light. I assure you I looked for Miriam everywhere.

I searched the whole of the pier head. Take my word for it. No, I didn't search the underneath, I wouldn't go down there. I told you about my vertigo. But I leaned over the rails of the sun deck and thought I saw boys fishing. I may have glimpsed a line or two out from the northern side. But I can't be sure. If Miriam had been down there, she would be back by now. Unless she's played another joke on me. You will agree I did the right thing in coming to wait with you. Here comes the rain again. A pretty heavy storm this one. This will make the people move.

Not many more to come back now: then I can go home. You're cosy in here with the rain rattling the roof. It's a bit like my greenhouse. The rain darkens the windows and frosts them over. I should go outside? Of course. How can I look for Miriam through a crying window pane? How clever of you to spot that. But I don't think she will come. And I might catch my death of cold out there for nothing. And what a wind. But it's worse at the end of the pier. Don't go down there where it's blowing a gale. Even the iron girders are creaking. They are drenched. The sea is sucking off the barnacles. How do they survive, clinging on like that? They are a Phenomenon of Nature; nothing else can cling like that.

The rain has stopped again.

I can see blue through the glass: Vanda Caerulea.

No one has passed this hut of yours for a good ten minutes now. Is it safe to assume that everyone has gone? The stragglers? Ah, the stragglers. We must wait for them: the fishermen, the ones from under the pier. Tomorrow you must forbid fishing under there. Meanwhile I worry about my wife, which is only natural, isn't it? Do you worry about yours? Everyone worries about his wife. They must do. They *are* a worry. Was that a scream?

It came from down there where the pier is fading in the dusk.

It was a Seagull. Nasty birds. They eat offal. As I walked back along the pier I saw them pecking mussels on the mud spit. Have they voracious appetites? Have they! Do they always feed on flesh? I should say they do, and greedily, until the bones alone remain. They are scavengers like the shell fish, transmuting what the sea has decomposed. Miriam was fond of shell fish. She ate them all. Now she has gone. Home? I wonder. At least I have your word that I waited here; that I waited here with you for a long time after first searching the pier. And you will vouch for this. You will say how long I waited here for Miriam. The storm has lifted. I must say farewell.

It has been pleasant talking to you here. I hope that you have understood. I must go home now to do a bit of clearing up. I have important things to do.

If Miriam isn't there, I'll be back.

Maggie Ross

The Special Pair

How to describe them . . .

Someone once said they had a look of collective self-possession which seemed to buttress them against the world. But neither now would enjoy being reminded of such a thing, although they must still both be aware that it was so.

Still they look so very much a couple that one finds it difficult after so long to think them separate. As always they look right together – a peculiar kind of matching which people say occurs between those who live together long – not so much a similarity of looks, like man and dog, or of mannerisms, like master and servant, but some secret mutual identity which nothing can quite destroy however hard the attempts.

That they have certain mannerisms in common is not altogether strange considering that it is now some fourteen years since they first met (although there is some mystery about the actual circumstances). There are those inflections of the voice that make one raise a knowing finger, say 'Ah!' and point towards the other one. Hear how he said that? Such a singular way of remarking it. She said the same thing yesterday, in the same way. They still do it. How can they help it, for no one has yet told either how frequently (still) he or she seems an identical twin. Now it is too late to say such things. But it pleases people to pigeon-hole, especially such a pair, as slippery as eels entwined, winding between your fingers, trying to foil you.

Once they had a disconcerting habit of communicating without words, even without the small gestures of brow and finger by which some reveal their secrets. They seemed to pick up each other's processes of thought like magic, as if the words had actually been spoken, continuing the conversation beyond the point that others thought it should be. Listeners would be mystified, wondering suddenly if perhaps they weren't getting old, or were unaccountably in the way. Of course it is understandable that after so many years there should be areas of collective information in which these two could perform their mental shorthand, but often they startled by the speed with which an idea passed from mind to mind. At times like these a look of pleased complicity would pass across each face, as if together they had performed quite exquisitely a difficult act of conjuring, the secret of which they would be keeping to themselves.

Perhaps it is untrue too, to say they do not look alike: many have remarked on a resemblance, although they may have noticed only a similarity of feeling expressed in both faces. Often the pleasure or anger of either could be seen mirrored in the other's face. Often they aped each other's expressions in order to achieve amusement, preferring anything to immobility. But on looking at them carefully there is something similar – about the set of the mouth, the way the eyes narrow when the listening is careful, the gestures of the hands when the thoughts are deep. Fashions in figures and faces change, these two remain fresco-drawn. She doesn't have his gentleness of movement, or he her nervousness, but each has that orphaned air peculiar to some Renaissance figure, luminous, outlined in an orange grove. In the past people have been fooled by this orphaned look, not suspecting that beneath the beautiful and mild exteriors there raged (or had the likelihood of raging) the fury of twin beasts. It was a joke to them, always a joke, that really – taking everything into account – they were such devilish fiends. That others were so easily taken in by such Botticelli sublimity, pleased them for, in their opinion, anyone with perspicacity should have known that here was double devilry.

Double it had to be, for if one opted out then the game was at an end and all pleasures gone. Together the black deeds were plotted, the dark thoughts discussed. What if the result was a mere trip to Woolworth's to steal a few cheap articles; or the construction of realistic five-pound notes to drop at the feet of gullible passers-by. . . . They prided themselves on being the manipulators. And with such faces they may have been successful. Perhaps they still are, each in his own way, although it seems doubtful that one could rise individually to the heights of two. And surely now neither would take pride in achievement when separated from the other's applause. Applause was always such a necessary appurtenance. Without the other to approve, each would become wary, afraid perhaps of failure; certainly afraid of the other's devilish smile. Knowing the extent of one another's powers, they did right to stay wary. Their expressed opinions on foolishness allied to failure, were scathing and destructive. They saw themselves together as invincible; as removed from reality as anything adorning the Uffizi walls.

Once, in a rare euphoric moment several years ago, they confided their collective image, shyly and with truthful faces. They said they were a special pair: their classicism was ageless, and yet cinematic – the phase then was all to do with cinema. Never had there been so much enthusiasm for black and white. They said they were the spiritual offspring of Cocteau. They said that really they were *Les Enfants Terribles*. He had written the story because of them, and for them, and for no one else. He must have known them in a former existence. It was a rare conjunction of fact and fiction, never again to be repeated. Not that they weren't full of criticism for the film's dialogue, the sentimental music, disapproval of the acting, carping at the sets; being generally able to put others off the genuine scent in the way expected of a pair of fledgling fiends. If total concentration upon themselves – a passionate interest in each other almost to the exclusion of anyone outside – satisfaction at what they saw, cunning, and intelligence wilfully misapplied were how they regarded Cocteau's offspring, then truly this pair were his with a vengeance.

Strange that these two joined by mere marriage, should see each other incestuously. Yet not so strange when one considers the passion of their involvement. If one thinks how numerous are the primitive tribes who link through mingling of the blood, then it is easier to see why these two should also wish for consanguinity. As brother and sister they were lovers; as relatives they were friends; as friends they were conspirators. And as enemies ... how long can they exist?

Like *Les Enfants Terribles* they indulged in silly ceremonies involving knives and flowers, both totally aware of the ridiculousness of their behaviour, both ready at the flicker of the first smile to throw over the entire affair and sit and laugh together at such stupidity. So much did each rely upon the other's approval and complicity, it would have been unthinkable to continue in the face of the smallest dissent.

Now if you went to them and mentioned Vivaldi, or poisoned mushrooms; a shadowy house with screens and high ceilings, they would be bound to open a cold, cold eye as if you had interrupted special thoughts with your chatter, and were therefore responsible for losing something of present value for the trivia of a long gone past. One of them at least (if not both) might now be capable of disowning such romantics, claiming you conjure out of context that which was, at best, no more than a passing moment in their lives and not (as is well known) their whole raison d'être for the length of an entire year.

A year. ... Perhaps it was more. But the stage was outgrown like stages before and stages since; each retaining something in them of the last, but moving almost mechanically to something new. And now it changes yet again, as it has done so many times before with them, slipping sometimes one small cog, sometimes turning an immense revolution – if revolution is the word for that which turns inexactly, never able to go back to where it started. Their relationship was never the stagnating kind: neither was capable of leaving well, or ill, alone. They wanted it that way, calling down the heavens on the head of anyone suggesting there might be peace in untroubled continuity. As if they didn't have, in their own way, the continuity they professed to hate, both unaware of this beautiful and simple fact until they found it threatened.

Boredom was the worst enemy: they ran from it as from the devil, frequently into a far worse state of ennui than before. To watch them wandering together hand in hand, the slothfulness of movement belied by the darting glances, was to know that within seconds of discovering novelty of any sort, they were capable of instant, explosive action. One might urge the other to test the validity of TRESPASSERS WILL BE PROSECUTED; the other dare to place himself among the guests outside the church, waiting to be immortalized within a wedding photograph. The real test came in prolonging the activity beyond the moment. It wasn't that they didn't recognize the meaning of such boredom, speaking about it with derision, but they liked to use what they considered was great intelligence in order to defeat it. In their opinion there was nothing about themselves they didn't know, until uncharted fragments broke and floated before their amazed eyes. Knowing the dilettante in themselves, they set about using it in their defence. Hadn't Beardsley been a bit like them? Romans galore ... Hippies ... Beatniks .. name them. Being so was a full-time job. If one recognizes that games are being played, then they must be played with all the energy one can muster, until the players are exhausted and all the possibilities along with them. No hungry man stuffing himself with food ever attacked with such relish. Yet they should have known that the famished may have to start feeding like a child if he is to keep down what he has eaten. When they were serious it meant no stoppage to the games, but rather a pleasant pause during which they said, 'Now we shall be serious for a while'; and so another cog slowly clicked into position. Often being serious meant only total application to whatever they were doing. There was devotion in the way they picked up things – objects appealing to the imagination which were handled lovingly, tenderly examined and discussed, then placed in the pockets as talismen. Why not? Les Enfants had done likewise, keeping all their treasures in a special drawer, hugging closely anything that came within the consideration of their own insularity.

Meetings with strangers were serious, and attractive: both were well aware that others might want inclusion in the magic circle. They recognized that kindred spirits might exist in a world peopled by millions, allowing that maybe a few – a very few – would be like them. During times of generosity they might make an effort to like whom they met, saying how good to feel such sympathy. Meetings occurred. Then, thinking how they recognized themselves, they would suddenly become alive, as if a hidden hand had switched on all the lights. It was good, briefly, to know the same language was being spoken. They talked about it, telling their feelings to the new, and slightly amazed friend. But as quickly the light could disappear, the friendship fade (unless that friend was super stoical). They realized, they said, that nobody would ever completely be capable of understanding them. And why should they attempt to understand the others? They had themselves. Let others come and try to join the magic circle for it was to revolve forever. And people always came, attracted by the orphaned look, and the pleasure promised. Friendship meant adjustments which they felt were well worth making, at the time, if only for the sake of novelty. For whoever the new friends, they would find themselves expected to supply sufficient entertainment to maintain their places in the action: they were expected to overcome the threat of calm.

Was it coincidence which made him bring home the girl during one of their quieter times, when boredom not only threatened but sometimes arrived and seemed to settle? They had begun to review their ages, trying for the first time to go beyond the games and see themselves again. They spoke about the idea that possibly age was changing them. It came to them distastefully that perhaps now they could not rightfully consider themselves as the children they had always been. How old were they then? Maybe twenty-four or five; still concerned with the things which Cocteau's children had outlived (or died) so fast. The girl didn't know she had come at crisis time. She knew nothing beyond the fact that her opinion was often asked. What did *she* think of growing old? Didn't she think it better to stay young? Neither of them had any intention of becoming ancient wrecks, a burden to themselves and others. She answered honestly, feeling the woman's challenge, and the man's attraction. She told them the time was right for turning thinking outward. Change was in the air. She knew by the small, chill smiles she drew she was considered female wise and, by the female, competition. He listened as she spoke, not hearing as she did her words turned banal in the hands of an expert. On several occasions he asked her home, wanting to hear what she had to say about behaviour, and society. Why shouldn't he work at something permanent for a change, instead of fading swiftly from job to job, she said. They told her no scene must interfere with travel plans – whether or not any journey was under consideration at that time. She did her best, trying to think of useful employment for such a chameleon. He wouldn't work at anything base, they said, although what they considered base was only a list of unconnected jobs, compiled (with hilarity) on the spot. He couldn't be a clerk . . . never. But mending roads was somehow noble. Archaeology was all the rage, and therefore to be avoided. Since Rat-catching was on the wane he might begin another vogue. Or maybe spend his time writing something startling – say, the memoirs of a twelve-year-old. At this they laughed with satisfaction, making her feel extraneous. There was no real need of finance, both being complacent recipients of the generosity of parents who had long since abrogated responsibility in any other areas.

Now he was to go to work in earnest. The girl had said so and he had listened. And she had had the sense to agree. It was her turn for dictatorship, sensing as she did that should their relationship continue unchanging in the presence of this other person, she might find herself in a different role. A terrible thought ... that instead of a lover in her bed she might one night find a son with confessions to make.

'I'm not your keeper,' she told him, in a tone of voice usually reserved for private speech. The girl kept quiet. She had already said too much. She had only come to be their friend. That she found herself loving him was coincidental and, by the time it happened, too late to put to rights. For the first time he treated the words as a challenge and went to look for work without her help. As always his job was to have been mutually approved and mutually chosen. The girl approved and helped him choose. And to make it worse he came home joyful.

That he should have so misjudged reaction seems to suggest that there were other areas not sufficiently recognized as private by these two who, for so long, owned that privacy with them was double.

Smiling, he ignored her first, small furies, saying things with a new clarity she found unbearable. Where was the complicity? Why did he too not turn his fury on the outsider? 'She is good,' he said. And, 'Leave her alone.' He knew too well what she was capable of. There was no kindness in him. He was too vehement and rapidly untouchable. She said she didn't trust him. Partially it was right, for he had begun the small lies necessary for his equilibrium. There was nothing she knew he wasn't capable of. To her questions he gave avoiding answers, because of fiendishness. The hysteria was slowly rising and about to engulf them both. In reality neither gave the other chance to speak the simple truth: for too long they had invented complication. Now as more words embroidered the air, they blocked the truth. When, in a moment of taunting, he said he loved the girl, the barrier was up. He didn't say how it pleased him to be treated with gentleness as a fascinating stranger. All he told her was that hers was not the only beauty, and how the girl's quiet sentences were more meaningful than her familiar avalanche of words. He saw himself in a new light in which there was room for another kind of self-deception. She told him so. Hardly listening, he smiled dissent. Slowly he was making separation, moving towards an approval attractively uncritical.

Whether or not the girl was waiting on the sidelines for the battle's outcome, wasn't clear. Of course her visits ceased. He said he wasn't seeing her. If he was to be believed. But she was always there; her presence hung among the darkening shadows, blinding them further when they had need of clear sight. Anger was overwhelming them – they who had once expressed surprise that it could last beyond the limits of two people in each other's arms at night.

Reprisal there had to be. He must be shown. In retaliation she found a man: someone sufficiently remote to be unaware of danger. He could have been anyone. She hadn't cared. He was to be used to right a wrong – Exhibit A for the Prosecution; a warning that two could play the same game. It isn't obvious whether she thought at all beyond the first few hours or days of this new love. There was no consideration of possible hurt to him; no fear that he might be strong enough to choose a different way. Fiends let loose against each other can do more harm in the space of two weeks than can gentle people all their lives. What did it matter to her if the man saw them as a happy future pair. She ignored his dreams, having seen the pattern set by Cocteau's children, and having approved it. He was a lamb led to the battleground, to be fought around until the pain of his wounds made him want to be free of such a pair of devils. Two weeks between the crossfire of their fury. And when he retired defeated his ghost lingered too, like the music of Vivaldi filling the house with jangling echoes; deafening them.

Neither had the strength to bear such powerful and recent memories. Neither knew an exorcism strong enough to give them what they most desired – a little individual peace. It was too late. They had set the patterns themselves. 'Why did you do it?' 'What was so wrong?' they shouted in unison, unable to hear the answering cries. There was no peace. That was the time of danger in those days of the threshing and the pain. She raged about the rooms, crying how she was suffocating because of him. Helplessly he called her names, and she believed them all. No more work for him and no more play for either. Now they were singular fiends removing themselves word by word from mutual protection. The bewilderment increased. And the violence.

If one walks slowly through the rooms, taking careful note of unusual marks on walls and furniture, one can see the extraordinary strength they used against each other: the half-moon of a whisky glass deeply indenting the woodwork of the dining-room door; plaster flaking above the bedroom mirror where the clock ticked its last. Luckily they always missed, swearing that they never intended to do otherwise, but sometimes cursing their bad marksmanship. She has been known to pick up all the sofa cushions one by one and throw them in staggering arcs across the room, knocking over everything en route. In the past he might have laughed as he caught a cushion and hurled it back, running to hug her for her terrible inaccuracy. Instead he watched her, waiting for her to appear as the woman he had known. Instead of wanting to hold her hand, now he might twist it from her wrist. She watched him, the violent words whipping them into frenzy. She stayed away from his swinging arm and the momentum of the madness, preparing to defend herself. In the kitchen his eyes would widen as he watched the carving knife in her hand deftly slicing chicken, or flicking the skin from the length of a cucumber, she smiling secretly as she worked. Then was not the time for dangerous repartee:

nothing inflammatory was ever spoken within range of kitchen carvers. The control was coming with difficulty, and was hard to learn.

How strange that they should have stayed together in such torment, when common sense told both of them to run alone and hide. Each seemed to hold a fascination for the other, as if each asked: 'What will he think of next?' 'How will she behave tomorrow?' The threats to leave, the cries of 'Whore' and 'Harridan' flung and shattered with the crockery became a part of their days and nights until all had been said not once but a thousand times, and the house resembled, in its bleakness, the home of Les Enfants. But energy was deserting them, as it had to finally. Gradually the abuse became more automatic; it had to. The days and nights were long. Fists were lowered, the cries subsided. They subsided into argument which sometimes had the power to burst into action for which each now was prepared. They had armoured themselves against each other, determined to continue fighting (for they were sure to find a way) until they reached conclusion.

Yet now, to hear their voices coming from another room, neither raised much above the level of conference, you would believe they were discussing nothing more unusual than the daily routine of rise, eat, entertain. The voices have been going on for so long that one could be lulled into thinking that nothing very much has changed. They rise and fall but are never silent for long except when one is absent, or sleep overtakes them. Listen closer and one can hear the reasons and replies, the descriptions and denials hour by hour, knowing by heart the likely variation. The smooth flow of their neurosis is now so much part of the house that if it were to cease one would feel the silence like the cut of the cold wind. The passionate games, the joyful resistance to reality have given way to the terrible pattern of the present.

How to describe them . . .

Ageing children overtaken by something they always

thought they could give the slip. . . . Two people like any other two, who live together; who live separately like any others. Two who cannot live apart because of a multitude of complexities into which they entwined themselves; who must watch each other for a long time to come before they are able to turn and look outward.

Maggie Ross

An Obsessive Act of Creation, or Destruction

A road. The mind goes back to it again. Almost despite oneself the mind goes back, moving along the lines of its formation and returning as if in its perspective there is perpetual motion. Its horizontals curve until they form a sphere magically self-contained – in its end its beginning. Like a bluebottle one hovers, searchlighting this and that, reflecting on the possibilities. They seem to be infinite, as infinite as the many roads there must be exactly resembling this one.

In reality it is two roads, one at right angles to the other. When one stops it is always at the intersection. Neither road seems very long, the three possibilites of view being cut off by a curve, a bend, a skyline, a group of trees, a block of insignificant shops, the tall fence of an unremarkable garden, all of which are noted and passed by in the returning. At the meeting of the two roads there is a school directly facing the second road, so that if one stands with one's back to the railing of the yard one can see the houses diminishing, and distant chimney pots of other houses in other roads.

But there seems no real reason for remembering, nothing to titillate the senses, unless what constitutes anonymity is worth consideration. Certainly here there is essence of banality which somehow still manages to be attractive and worthwhile. Perhaps it is something special about the light – always the same – which begins as twilight or a certain sort of yellowness suggesting night is not too far away. As one watches the yellow deepens into grey, until the specific becomes blurred impression and the impressions fade until all that are left are silhouettes against a white night sky. This timelessness means there are no seasons, although plane trees grow in their squares of dog-soiled earth, garden hedges thicken as they age. There are leaves sometimes on the pavements and tree bark lies like dandruff in the gutters. Change is here but nothing changes. No violence can be done to the idea of a road . . .

There is the sound of leaves rustling. There is air. To be breathed. There are people in the road. Two. Only two at present: male and female, arm in arm approaching the intersection. And far away so faint as to be merely a murmur on the wind the sound of something like traffic, or the rumbling of thunderous muffled winds. He is limping and trying half-heartedly to free himself from the wiry grip of her hand. Beyond these two people who are stopping beside the railings of the school is the sound of the city, breathing and rumbling and murmuring. If they looked up they could see their own special familiar landmarks. They look at the young man's foot which he has raised delicately gazelle fashion while he complains about the pain.

She shakes his arm gently. 'We're here.'

'So what?'

Considering how frequently this dialogue has been performed it is surprisingly difficult to reproduce. It varies. Sometimes it is full of hidden humour and quite spirited, at others there is peevishness and a sense of being thwarted. Now they stand coldly while he clings to the railing with one hand, the other grappling with his shoelace.

'Strange it should happen right here . . .'

'Very. But it has.'

'I'd like to know what's actually happened anyway . . .'

His shoe is off. But the sock is troublesome having stiffened either through lack of washing or some foreign agent. The ritual is always the same: with difficulty he removes the sock, then they both look closely at his foot. His face twists with pain, hers with doubt. She isn't sure that an issue isn't being dodged by this behaviour. She releases her hand as a kind of protest.

'Don't you want to go after all?'

'It's my toe . . .'

'Because if you don't then I'm going home. It's already six-thirty.'

'Fifteen. It's my toe.' The white foot dangles as if dead. A drop of very red blood suddenly colours the pavement. Another falls.

'You're bleeding!'

'Observant!'

'It's your toe.'

'I know.'

'Why is it bleeding?'

'I always bleed from the toe in September.'

Since there is no real reason why he should be bleeding from the toe, this reason is good enough. It has happened to people.

Politely she smiles at his joke and offers a scrap of handkerchief. But he prefers to dab at his foot with his sock.

'Is there a hole in your shoe?'

After peering into its darkness and gingerly putting a hand inside he thinks not. There is no consideration here of the state of his shoes, although this might seem to have some bearing on the affair. The state of their entire clothing has not been studied. They could be wearing anything. Everything. Or nothing.

'Something sharp got me. Like a glass.'

'Have you walked on any lately?'

'How do I know? All I do is walk. Minding my own business. May have been glass. May not.'

This time there is going to be lack of sympathy between them.

They look down and see the red drop has enlarged again.

'It's my blood.'

'There's nothing to be afraid of. Everybody's got it.'

'But most people manage to keep it inside them.'

She sighs. 'If you're going to stand here like a crane I'm going.' She moves past the open gate of the school playground. 'I don't think you really wanted to come at all.'

'I don't like it,' he says.

'It was just big ideas.' She nods towards the school door. There are steps, and a blackboard on which are chalked the words: EVENING CLASSES. ENROLMENT TONIGHT – LANGUAGES.

'I don't like the repetition.' He stared at his blood as though mesmerized. 'It happened once before ... my toe bled.'

'You have a weakness.' For her the subject is now closed. She seems to be demonstrating here the female trait of using incisiveness as the subjugator of fear.

'No! It was my father's toe! I remember him telling it. He said he got weak from loss of blood.'

At this point one is aware of other people. The girl notices them. She sees a figure running across the end of the road opposite. But by the time her eyes are used to the shadows the figure has gone, and the momentary alarm it caused has subsided. It is getting darker. Rooftops which earlier had been clearly defined are now settling under a light mist or smoke which lessens colour and blurs edges. It seems to be invading the tops of trees, clouding the blackness of unlit windows and closed doors. Even hedges are turning grey. Another figure follows the first, not so much running as sidling with great urgency. She looks harder in case he is followed by a third. No one. She thinks she sees a faint column of distant smoke in the sky.

'Where is everybody?'

'I'm here,' he says. He is rubbing blood smears from his hand with the sock. The pool of blood on the pavement is now saucer size. He shows her his palms and laughs without amusement.

'I'll live I suppose. We always do! We never quite bleed to death!'

Sometimes he says only youthful things and sometimes he is capable of what passes for wisdom.

He looks at her and wonders why her head is cocked like a bird. He sees her listening and listens too. He hasn't seen the people running across the end of the opposite avenue.

Here a break occurs during which the bleeding stops, the sock and shoe are replaced and he gives vent to a collection of words in the form of a condensed lecture. Since nobody else is there to listen, the lecture must be for the girl's benefit although her interest is marginal, her attention polarized between the need to get him inside the school gate, and the likelihood of other people fleeing through the trees.

'Is today a festival?' she says.

He doesn't care. He dislikes being interrupted in full intellectual flow. He wishes to discourse on the need for education. He speaks about it and people, saying how necessary it is to them before they can get to know about each other. They should learn each other's ways. And languages. There should be an educational system whereby this can be achieved. He has a plan – a five-year plan which soon he will commit to paper. But first he will put it to the test himself by learning a language – any language – and using this language to help him learn another. And so on, until the plan becomes a new way of life and the years have passed in study and good works.

Sometimes it seems preferable that he should say nothing while he replaces his sock and shoe, standing on one leg and concentrating his entire self on the operation, while the girl exhorts him to hurry in case he loses his place in the new class. Perhaps the class is her idea, although it doesn't matter. What matters more is that they have mentally turned their backs upon each other. Now he has turned his on the road. He hasn't noticed how she looks in amazement at the distant trees suddenly alive with running men and women who dash across the road and disappear, sometimes colliding with each other in their haste.

'Twenty-eight . . . twenty-nine . . . thirty . . .' She is counting them. She stands in the gutter to get a better view, squinting through the foggy light. She sees them slip between the trees like paper knives.

'Look!'

Their speed is furtive. Their legs move but make no sound. There are no cries or shouts. In the air is the drone of distant traffic or machinery which now seems louder in the gathering dusk. The people move fast with hunched shoulders, carrying the burden of the evening; uniformly grey, uniformly faceless. It would make no difference to the road if they weren't there: their presence would be sensed or felt, like the smoke which swirls but isn't tangible and has no smell.

Then footsteps. The boy turns and sees three women – elderly – already in the school yard and making for the steps as fast as their old legs will allow. They are pointing at the enrolment board.

'I must go,' he says.

From now on there is an inevitability about events which gives them always the same sequence and the same momentum.

'Do you hear me?'

But she is hearing something else. 'Machines,' she says. She cannot see now beyond the first few trees of the opposite avenue but she knows there is confusion.

Hastily he ties his laces. 'Why don't they put the street lights on?'

An old man with a stick has arrived at the school gate. He reaches it before the boy and taps towards the step. In his hand is a booklet: *Adult Education.*

'What's the matter?'

The girl can hear machines which rumble and drone like giant bluebottles. The air is filling with increasing sound which billows down through the trees and where the houses were and fills the spaces left by the running people. The people have gone and the sound is separating into recognizable and frightening disharmonies. She can hear aircraft. She can hear the sound of splintering, and cobbles being crushed under the weight of vehicles.

Inside the school a light comes on, each window a sudden yellow square. The girls turns and her frightened face is lit. It looks as though it is on fire.

'I'm going,' the boy calls.

Her mouth moves as if she is saying something like 'You mustn't,' or 'You shouldn't.' But he doesn't hear. He gives a tiny reluctant shrug because she doesn't follow him, then walks towards the steps. When he looks again she is staring at him and shaking her yellow head.

'It was your idea!' But she cannot hear. He shrugs again and joins two middle-aged men who are going into the building.

Now the girl stands with her back to the school fence looking up the dark avenue opposite. She waits, rigidly upright, staring towards the direction of a single sound which has separated from the rest. She can hear the squeak and rattle of heavy wheels confined by caterpillar treads. She can hear a tank coming down the road towards her. Two circles of bright light emerge between the trees. The tank is advancing fast. She steps back on to the pavement; still watching, seeing the lights grow large until they become attached to the blackness which is the vehicle and she can see its size; the way it is tearing a swathe through the trees. She sees the branches rip and fall. She sees them crush beneath the metal treads and lie in the rutted road. She sees the guns. She has stepped back as far as she can go. Somebody has closed the school gate. The school door is shut.

For a moment longer she hesitates, looking frantically from left to right. The tank is nearly at the intersection. She looks at the pavement beneath her feet. She is standing beside a pool of drying blood. The noise is terrible. The girl gets down on her knees. She sees the tank entering the area of yellow light. Carefully she lies down on the pavement. She lies on her back, arms at her sides, arranging her head carefully so that it lies just beside the pool of blood. She closes her eyes. She waits.

Robert Nye

The Same Old Story

The treasurer is the guardian of the fabric. It'll be Maddy then. Maddy's been everywhere and done most things. Travelling across Europe he sees a woman in the lower berth undressing. She takes off her wig and her false breasts, she removes her glass eye. As she is unfastening her cork leg she notices Maddy. What do you want? she says. You know what I want, says Maddy, unscrew it at once and throw it up here. It's Maddy's job to see that the font is full of water and the incense up to scratch. It's his duty to supply bread and wine for the eucharist, and he orders such little matters as the ringing of the bells. His stall is opposite the chancellor's. The chancellor's name is Knox. Knox has Visionary stamped on his forehead. He falls asleep outside the alehouse once. He's drunk and his little pal is hanging out. Two of the choirboys come by and tie a red ribbon on it. When Knox wakes up and sees the ribbon he says to his penis: God knows where you've been or what you've been up to, but I'm glad you won first prize. Don't confuse Knox with the chancellor of the diocese, Coverdale. Knox is charged with the oversight of the cathedral school. It's also his task to correct slovenly readers. In some cathedrals the chancellor is the secretary of the chapter. Knox is not. He sits in the easternmost stall, on the dean's side of the choir. The dean's name is Pulex. He sits first on the right on entering the choir at the west, the chief stall. Trumper sits in the corresponding stall on the left-hand side. Trumper is the precentor. He baked a cake once in honour of the Virgin's lying-in. Pulex wouldn't have it. No such ceremony should be observed, he pointed out, because she suffered no pollution, therefore needed no purification. Trumper is a sentimentalist. He leans towards Rome. Last summer he told two of the choirboys that Lady's Thistle gets its name from the fact that Our Lady, walking from Leith with aching breasts, shook or squirted drops of milk upon it, to relieve the tension. The lads were kind not to report this opinion to the dean. It's true that the leaves of the plant are diversified with white spots. Trumper is always going on about Jesus's mother. Whether it's her virginity, her sinlessness, or her peculiar closeness to the Godhead, the present writer is not sure, but something about the woman appeals to him greatly. He won't even have it that the brethren of Our Lord were Joseph's children by a former marriage. Their mother was quite another Mary, he says, Mary the wife of Clopas or Alphaeus, the Virgin's sister. Knox says that the colourlessness of Mary's character, not only in the gospels but in the apocrypha too, makes it fatally easy to imagine her and to imagine one understands that imagination. Trumper ignores this thorn. He bought a kitten in the fish-market and christened it Dulia. When Knox heard him calling it, he said what do you call that cat? Dulia, said Trumper. After the martyr? said Knox. No, not Julia, Dulia, Trumper explained. I hear you now, said Knox, and added, I thought you had a cold. When the cat got bigger Trumper started calling it Hyperdulia. It was a fat cat, kink-tailed, tabby in colour, forever shaking its head as if it wanted to lick its ear, a nasty sort of creature. It had fleas, and the fleas gave it worms. The flea-larvae swallow the eggs of the worm along with the organic matter in the bottom of the cat-box. The worm-larvae hatch from these eggs in the midgut of the flea-larvae, penetrate the midgut and arrive in the stomach of the flea-larvae. They stay there during the pupal and adult stages of the flea, growing all the while. An animal becomes infected or re-infected by swallowing such fleas when, for example, licking its coat. Dulia was always licking her coat, so she was forever eating her own fleas and giving herself worms. Knox referred to this as a vicious circle or at least circumlocution, cat licking, cat chewing, fleas going down, worms breeding in the swallowed fleas, cat having worms, flea-larvae eating the eggs of the worms along with the organic matter in the bottom of the cat-box, cysticercoids hatching in the midgut, and so on, and so on, adult fleas copulating a few hours after their emergence from the cocoon and before having had a blood meal, the females laying a batch of fresh eggs after a day or two, but needing a blood meal before each batch. Trumper liked his cat. Perhaps he did not love it, but he liked it.

It's Maddy's job to report on the damage, being treasurer and guardian of the fabric. He doesn't have a great deal to report. A fragment of stone from one of the Norman arches in the south transept fell to the floor, killing a mouse. The pinnacles at each of the four angles of the central tower have cracks in them, but that was done before, although a certain amount of dust seems to be coming down from near the apex of the one to the south west, and that is new. The finial of the pinnacle of the Lady Chapel is dislodged. All three pinnacles at the western front testify to a minor disturbance. Mr Gore, the ecclesiastical sculptor, who clambered up across the lead roofing of the nave to assess the damage, reckons that they have been shifted about the length of a man's finger. The pinnacles are within thirty yards of the top window of the present writer's workroom. He has just been inspecting them through binoculars. In his opinion, the central pinnacle has been rotated clockwise, perhaps two inches, no more. The northern pinnacle is still less slightly rotated the other way, a mere half inch. The southern pinnacle appears to have undergone no rotation at all, but may be horizontally disturbed. Maddy, having spoken to Mr Gore's mason, who repaired the caps of these pinnacles about twelve years ago, suggests that all three of them are rotated in the same direction, that is, anti-clockwise. But Maddy repels by his manner. He's anxious and cow-like, both at once. Serving two masters, he's bound to lie to one of them. He has bright little black eyes and drinks like a fish on the quiet. He's always at the communion wine. It's his job to look after things like that, so naturally he buys the bottles and keeps the key to the cupboard. The stuff's endlessly watered down. He can't leave it alone. Just let the dean turn his back and Maddy's in the cupboard with the cork out. Pulex doesn't suspect a thing. He takes people at their face value, and his treasurer always looks sober. Besides, Maddy often talks about the perils of drunkenness. Not so often as to make it apparent that the subject fascinates him, but just enough to convince the dean he has a horror of it. His favourite story is of the hermit to whom the devil came disguised as another hermit, asking what did he think was the greatest sin? Self-love, says the hermit. Ha ha, says the devil. Incest, says the hermit. Try again, says the devil. Imagination, says the hermit. Not at all, says the devil, it's Red Hackle. The hermit won't believe him, so the devil takes him along to a pub, pays for his dram, and disappears. The hermit drinks the place dry. He's absolutely plastered, blind to the world. On the way home to his cell, he meets a beautiful girl. Quick as a flash, he's got his john thomas out and he's showing it to her. Half-a-crown, he says, if you rub this for me. Rub it yourself, says the girl, for nothing. The hermit does. The girl watches. Then the hermit kills the girl because she's seen his sin. He has to kill the witness to his sinning. As it happens, the beautiful girl is the devil in disguise, but of course our fellow doesn't know this. He has now committed three mortal sins in one day, as Maddy always points out when he tells this tale, so he goes to a priest and confesses: drunkenness, indecency, and infraction of the sixth commandment, pretty bad. The priest refuses to absolve him. He sends him to the Pope, in Rome. When the Pope hears our hermit's confession he says, go home, stay in your cell, wear no clothes, speak no word, whatever happens. This is the hermit's only hope of being redeemed. He does as he is told. Five years later, Lady Haystack comes riding by. Lady Haystack is the natural daughter of Francis Joseph, Emperor of Austria. She is tall, thin, and brown, reminding one of a colt. Her hounds drive our fellow out of doors. He has hair all over his body, otherwise he is naked, with long cracked black nails and his beard wound round and round his neck like a scarf. Who are you? says Lady Haystack. He answers nothing. She prods him with her whip. He doesn't respond. She fetches him a sharpish one across the buttocks, ties him to her horse so he has to trot along behind as best he can, and takes him home. Lady Haystack keeps our hermit in her deerpark. Fifteen years he's there. At night he creeps into the pigsty with a flute and gets the pigs to polk to his music, but this is his only memory of what it was ever like to be a man. By day he is her animal, her creature. She whips him silly, which amuses everyone. He has to attend to her least function. Not a word passes his lips. Many of her friends say how intelligent he is, for a beast of burden. He's grim and hanging, living off husks, his shoulder-blades like broken wings. At last one morning an angel appears, just after he's suffered a particularly enthusiastic beating at the hands of her ladyship's grooms. Brother Claudius, the angel calls, Brother Claudius, you are delivered. At once the hair falls from the hermit's body. He is a man again. Lady Haystack gives him a hat and listens to his story. She begs his forgiveness, which he gives. Thereafter she treats her creatures less cruelly, lest she be entertaining a holy man all unawares. As for Brother Claudius, he goes back to his cell and lives a good life to the end, with never a drop of alcohol passing his lips. That is Maddy's favourite story. If it's not a very good story then take it that that is the point. If anyone loves Maddy, they love him deeply, all in all or nothing at all. The present writer agrees that he boils at a different temperature before leaving the subject. It should be enough to say that in the circumstances the treasurer's anti-clockwise seems capricious, also that the fractures are undeniably horizontal, about five feet from the apex in the central pinnacle, and about three feet from the apex in the other two.

The top windows of your author's workroom confront other windows, and above them a stucco cornice. It is only by standing on a footstool and leaning out recklessly across the sill that he is able to inspect the pinnacles on the western front of the cathedral, the pinnacles in question. The other pinnacles he cannot see at all. In the window immediately opposite a young couple have a bright green window-box full of scarlet geraniums. The window has muslin curtains with pink bands. Intimate and disturbing sounds come from this window. Below is the row: the fruit shop, the fish shop, the clock shop, next to that the grocer's, then the stationer's. The row has no roadway. In winter it is perfect with snow, because of the absence of traffic; only the baker's boy, powdered from top to toe and tottering under an enormous superincumbent weight of rolls, walks along it. In spring you can imagine a pregnant housemaid on her knees scrubbing the doorsteps. In summer it's all alive with the children of misery. Outside the grocer's a band of juvenile pickpockets is absorbed in pitch-and-toss. At a short distance, a motley crew busies itself in games of barley-break, blow-point, loggats, marbles, muss. Oaths and idiot laughter mark their play. They spit and cheat. Ginger is drunk and Jill adjusts her garters. Hal writes on Nelson with a knife. Pretty Victoria farts. Ace picks his teeth with a matchstick. It is still early, but the sun, who at this season takes only a nap, has got his chin above the level of the house-top opposite, where sparrows . . .

Enough of that. The fact that the geraniums fire red darts at your author's eyes is no excuse for him wishing himself someone else. The row is all right. He likes it. The row is sufficient place to be. The top windows of his workroom give a good view of the cathedral. The pinnacles are about thirty yards away, on a level with him. They can be quite clearly seen without recourse to a footstool, small or otherwise, or leaning on the sill, dangerous or otherwise, so he doesn't know why he lied like that, why he had to offer that particular lie. It gets boring when you lie, and more boring when you accuse yourself of lying, when you wonder if the original statement was a lie, or the accusation of lying a lie, and then realize the pathetic flick at honesty implied in putting it all down, worrying your head over the whole thing, lie, counter-lie, truth, imbalance, balance, this whole damned trick of delicacy, this whole business or stamp of susceptibility, words, hesitations, qualifications, definitions, withdrawal, what the present writer is trying to get away from. In a word already said: sensibility. Sensibility a curse. Melodramatic? Try again. Sensibility a nuisance. That's enough.

The spire of St Martin's Church, already weakened by the gale, is cracked right through about twelve feet from the apex, the upper portion being shifted bodily out of place. Hartree, the senior partner in the firm of architects entrusted with the church's repair, says that three pinnacles are also cracked right through, and the upper portions shifted to one side. A small finial of one of the pinnacles at the east end of St Nicholas's Church fell, as well as a portion of a pinnacle on St Peter's Church. Hartree sucks the rim of his hat as he looks at you. He has had an interesting life. When he was about sixteen he ran away from home and went into partnership with a man who made phosphorus boxes. Hartree's part in the business was the selling of these boxes. A piece of phosphorus was stuck in a tin tube, the match was dipped into the phosphorus, and it would ignite by friction. Such simplicity. Hartree was very fond of these boxes. He considered them a boon. He did not at all mind selling them. He was a good salesman too, quick in phrase, apt in gesture, not averse to disputation but stinkingly polite. One may imagine that he made his customers feel better than themselves; doubtless that's the trick of it. One day he was hawking his boxes as usual, in the market-place, on a flat stone under the town clock, which probably stood at five to eleven, it usually did, in those days, the sun spilling on the cobbles, white as salt, and quite a crowd gathered to watch him, from the bull ring, when the constable approaches. Are you selling? says the constable. I am selling, says Hartree. Do you have a licence? says the constable. Hartree shows it to him. The constable barely looks at it. He flicks it back at our friend as though he's frightened it might scratch his eyes if he holds it too close. Those phosphor boxes, he declares, are wicked things, calculated to encourage and assist thieves and burglars. Fiddle de dee, says Hartree. This is not at all the right thing to say to the constable. I say they are an abomination, the constable shouts, putting his face down next to the pedlar's. Sixpence, says Hartree, to you, comrade. The constable seizes him by the scruff of the neck, kicks his boxes into the gutter, and hauls him off before the magistrate. They don't go to court. No, the constable takes Hartree to the beak's own private house, on a hill, out of town. It's a big house, with a thick privet hedge and lawns like manicured butter. The beak's not pleased to see Hartree, and his temper does not improve when he hears what our friend has been up to. Those boxes, he declares, ought not to have been invented. You are a scoundrel, sir, to be endangering life and limb by selling them in a public place. How would you feel, he adds, if a child took it into his head to play with one of them, and caught fire, and burned to death? Hartree thinks carefully. He likes riddles. He is not good at them, but he likes them. He stands on his head to warm his wits. He hums and haws a while, playing on his lips with his forefinger. Come, sir, the magistrate thunders, my question is clear enough, is it not? How would you feel if a child burned to death because of one of your iniquitous phosphor boxes? Regretful, says Hartree. How dare you, says the beak. Hartree supposes that he has made an incorrect response again. Mortified! he screams, while the beak's face grows longer and blanker. He's a monster, says the constable. He should be in jail, the dirty bugger, and that's the long and short of it. A man like this is a menace to society, a threat to the sanctity of the individual, he adds. Hold on, says Hartree, all I've done is sell a few phosphor boxes at a bob a nob. Trmph, says the magistrate, then you plead guilty? A month. Hartree goes green. Are you sending me to prison? he asks. That I am, says the magistrate, a month's worth, to mend your ways, I hope you see the error of them. I'm more concerned about the error of yours, says Hartree, bold as brass. I consider these proceedings illegal, he explains. Indeed, says the magistrate. Indeed, says Hartree. Two months, says the magistrate. He writes it down on a piece of paper which he takes from a steel filing cabinet. He gives the paper to the constable. Hartree opens his mouth. Then he shuts it again. In Norwich prison he associates with the rest. If he had been inclined to turn thief, he says, he had plenty of opportunities and offers of instruction. The separate or silent system was not in vogue then. Hartree works on the treadmill. One day a fellow inmate approaches him in the yard. Good morning, says the stranger, whose name is Mr Nap, good morning and here is my recipe for a long and happy life: be bold, be bold, but not too bold. Hartree intimates by a shake of the whiskers that he does not understand this. The stranger marches beside him in the line out for exercise. As he marches he talks. He tells from the side of his lopsided mouth the following story: There was once a young lady called Lady Mary who had two brothers called Forbes and Edward. My name is Forbes. I was the elder brother! The Lady Mary, rest her soul in paradise, for she was my very sister and never a sweeter girl pulled on a pair of stockings! Attend, sir, to my tale. Our parents had been killed in the wars, for this was in a foreign country, but the new king was kind to us children and we were rich, owning houses in the north, the south, the east and the west also. When we grew up and came of an age to know our minds we chose to spend a little of each year in each house. Thus, in spring, we went to the house in the north. In summer, we went to the house in the east. In autumn, we went to the house in the south. And in winter, sir, in winter we went to the house in the west. Each house was adequate in its season. Lady Mary and my brother Edward and I were happy to travel and pleased to have four places to stay. For when one has travelled then it is good to stay, and when one has stayed a while then it is good to travel. What a satisfactory arrangement life is! Attend, sir. I have completed the preliminaries. The story proper begins. The house in the west was our favourite house. It stood on a blue cliff overlooking the sea. One winter, as soon as we were arrived there, we decided to hold a ball to which all the people round about could come. Lady Mary penned the invitations. My brother Edward and myself saw to it that there would be plenty to eat and drink, as well as Strauss for the dancing. The guests came, sir, and a merry evening began. Among the guests one man stood out. His name was Lord Fox. He was tall and dark, with a wit like a greengage. Nobody knew much about him. He was new to the west, they said. It was clear that he was not married and that he took a great fancy to my sister. Well he might. He danced with her till dawn, and saved all his choicest epigrams for her ears alone. Those ears were like snowballs, sir, delicate whorls of intricacy, like sliced snowballs, or mushrooms opened for the inspection of an elf. They were surpassed only by the beauty of her navel, though I say it myself. Be that as it may, the Lady Mary, my sister, was charmed by the company of Lord Fox. She was charmed, sir, and Edward was charmed, and I, Forbes, was also charmed. We were all charmed. Lord Fox came back again and again to the house on the cliff. It was a strange thing, as Lady Mary soon noticed, but we never needed to send him an invitation. Forbes has only to mention Lord Fox's name to Edward, she said, or Edward has only to say something to Forbes about Lord Fox, and there he is, there he will be, strolling towards us across the lawn in sunlight peeling off his elegant black mittens or leaning in the doorway toying with the hilt of his sword, nodding and smiling and wishing us good day. As for my sister herself, she had only to think of Lord Fox, and lo, he appeared. He dined with us, hunted with us, sailed with us in the bay and went with us for long walks on the shore looking for shells and starfish, which latter he likened to the dropped gloves of angels. His supply of amusing remarks was endless. He seemed to have been everywhere and done most things. For all that, he remained a somewhat mysterious personage. Edward and I never quite found out from his conversation who he was or where he came from – and he avoided our questions on points like these by telling us new stories, always so interesting and extraordinary that we quite forgot he had not answered us until later, when we began to feel unsatisfied and uneasy that we knew so little about him. But our sister, the Lady Mary, did not let such matters bother her. She found Lord Fox the most entrancing person she had ever met, and she was always asking him to visit our house on the cliff. One evening, towards Christmas, when Edward and I were busy in the armour room, Lord Fox turned to Lady Mary and said, it has been so pleasant all these times, visiting you here in your house, I feel I would be delighted to return the compliment. He had this rather cavernous way of speaking, which Lady Mary considered perfect in a gentleman. Why, sir, she said, what do you mean? I mean, said Lord Fox, smoothing his black moustaches, that you should come one day, my dear, and visit me in my house. Lady Mary felt a shiver trickle down her back. She dismissed the warning without giving it a thought. That would be most agreeable, she said, I'm sure that Forbes and Edward. . . . Oh no, Lord Fox said quickly, not Forbes, splendid fellow though he is, nor Edward, though I like to think of him as my own brother. Just yourself, dear lady. But I go everywhere with my brothers, protested Lady Mary. Just so, said Lord Fox. He smiled his most extreme smile and my sister felt her heart begin to melt. You should do some things on your own, my dear, he said. You aren't a child any more, you know, he reminded her. Lady Mary felt there was some truth in these remarks, but she promised nothing. Where is your house anyway, Lord Fox? she said. It's called Bold House, isn't it? I remember sending your invitation there, she added, but I'm not sure I've ever seen the place. Bold House, said Lord Fox, his black eyes sparkling, that's right, my dear.

Well, said Lady Mary, where is Bold House? Oh, you can't miss it, said Lord Fox, waving his vague white hand gracefully in the air. Nobody who comes to visit me ever misses it, he added. Lady Mary was puzzled. But which direction is it from here, she asked. North of the north, said Lord Fox, east of the east, south of the south, and west of the west. That sounds a long way, said Lady Mary. Not at all, said Lord Fox, in fact, you'd be surprised how near it is, my darling. Well, sir, just at that moment Edward and I returned and Lord Fox said no more to my sister about visiting his house. But the next time he came, and the next, he asked her again to visit him. He always waited until they were alone before suggesting it, and he always gave the same mysteriously vile directions. Lady Mary said nothing to us, her brothers, about any of this. Christmas Day arrived, and my sister found herself left on her own while Edward and I went flying hawks that had been given us by our aunts. She was bored and lonely, was the Lady Mary, and she fell to thinking about Lord Fox's invitations. How agreeably sinister they seemed! Her cockles quivered in her marrowbone! She decided to go and visit him. She put on her best blue dress and hat, and set out alone. Really, she did not expect to arrive anywhere. It seemed so hard to find a house that was north of north, east of east, south of south, and west of west. But the mystery was a challenge, so she tried. As it happened, sir, she found Bold House in no time at all. It was quite near, just as Lord Fox had said it was. Lady Mary could not understand how she had never noticed it before. It was a big house, and it had a black door. Lady Mary went up to the door and knocked. No one answered. Lady Mary knocked again. The doorknocker was cold in her hand. There was still no answer. Lady Mary noticed that over the portal of the door some words were written. She read them. The words said: Be bold, be bold, but not too bold. She knocked a third time. This time, sir, the black door swung slowly open. There was nobody there. Lady Mary thought to herself that the door could not have been properly bolted, which meant that perhaps Lord Fox was at home but had not heard her knocking. So she went in. The hall was long, and as cold as a tomb. Lady Mary passed down it, along it, through its cold length. She drifted past the wafting tapestries. Those tapestries had a life of their own. They moved, they writhed. The carpets were like snakes. My sister glided down the twilit corridors, pale, white as salt, like a ghost with a lamp in her hand. She passed the portraits of other sisters. She sped down carpetless corridors, by bare whitewashed walls. She was in a hospital interior, its dead veins leading towards a pumped-out heart. Her slippered feet were quaint on the chilling tiles. Her toes were benumbed, her ringless fingers aching each by each. At last she came to a spiral stair. As far as she had fallen through the house, so many levels had she now to climb. Over the stair some words were written. Lady Mary read them. The words said: Be bold, be bold, but not too bold. Lord Fox, called Lady Mary, 'tis I, Lady Mary. 'Tis myself, the Lady Mary. Cooee, haloo, greetings, she added, anybody home, Lord Fox? There was no answer. Lady Mary went slowly up the stair. Her dress was spread, so, on the ivory steps. They were long steps, alternate black and white, like piano keys, save that piano keys of course are not alternate. Well, sir, neither was the spiral ivory stair. It was arranged even as a keyboard is arranged, or even as a keyboard has been arranged since Virdung got to work on it. The Lady Mary climbed three octaves towards silence. Her trailing dress ascended through the dusk. Her train was a glissando, her golden hair a rallentando. There was music. At the top of the stair, sir, she came to a gallery. It was roofed with ice, like the inside of a wolf's mouth. The gallery was like a mouth anyway, agape. Over the entrance, above the entrance to the gallery, some words were written. The Lady Mary read them. The words said: Be bold, be bold, but not too bold. Crank, thought Lady Mary, can he really have the same idiot inscription written all over his house? Lord Fox, she called, where are you, Lord Fox? There was no answer. The listening house stood still. Lady Mary went on through the gallery. The walls glistened with frost. Her skirts made a swishing sound. At the end of the gallery she came to another door. This door was also black. But it was very small. There were some words written on it. Lady Mary had to kneel to read them. Her pince-nez slipped down her nose. Her suspenders twanged on her lithe brown legs. The words said: Be bold, be bold, but not too bold, lest that your heart's blood should run cold. The Lady Mary was not a person to be frightened off now that she had come so far. She turned the key in the tight lock. She opened the door. She stuck her head and shoulders into the tiny room. The tiny room was full of tubs of blood. Skeletons hung from hooks in the rafters. Skulls grinned at her from every shelf. The floor was thick with coils of human hair. Lady Mary did not scream. She shut the door. She stood up. She went to the window for air, and saw Lord Fox. He was coming towards the house across rank lawns. It had begun to snow and his figure, dressed all in black, loomed like a devil in a mist of whirling white flakes. He snowed towards my sister. He was whirling. He carried a thin sword in his left hand. With his right he dragged a young girl by the hair. The girl screamed. But Lord Fox said nothing. The Lady Mary sprang back from the window. She snatched up her skirts and ran through the gallery. She tried door after door for a place to hide, but all were locked. She hurried down the spiral stair. She flew. She spun. She fell. She glided. Her skin was the colour of mushrooms. Down the black and white, white and black stair she went, note after note after note after note. What was the tune, what was the melody of the Lady Mary's fall? It was the opening bars of *Death and the Maiden*, second movement, *andante con moto*, what else. It was the sound of a snowflake falling, the world in the evening, the dwarfs shouting *achtung*, the end of it all, minutest quickening conclusion. As she fell the last act rose to meet her. They met. They merged. They melted. Her hair streamed. Her shadow was a gleam on gleaming ivory. She could hear Lord Fox coming. She hid herself under the staircase. Lord Fox entered the hall. Lord Fox and his victim. My sister's heart was beating like a drum. A goitre like a bladder of lard, a goitre like a bladder of lard, bladder of lard, bladder of lard, bladder of bladder of bladder of lard, cried the heart of Lady Mary. It thought she must be caught. But Lord Fox did not see her. No, sir, yes, sir, so bent is he on his own cruel business that he does not see my sister where she lies huddled in the blue pool of her dress. He begins to drag the poor girl up the stair. The girl does not go easy. She screams. She kicks. She plunges. Begging for mercy, she catches hold of a knob at the turn of the banisters. Lady Mary, peeping up from her hiding place, sees the girl's hand tighten. The girl wears a silver bracelet round her wrist. As Lady Mary watches, Lord Fox raises up his sword and cuts off the girl's hand. Cut. Hand and bracelet fall in Lady Mary's lap. She hears Lord Fox going down the gallery, and the dragging sound of the girl behind him. The grand piano of the stair was silent. My sister ran, sir, ran ran ran from Bold House, ran through the snow, and did not stop running until she reached the safety of our house on the cliff. They had reached the end of the exercise period. Hartree turned to Mr Nap. An extraordinary story, he said. Mr Nap turned away. He said nothing. He went to his cell. All the rest of that day, and all night, Hartree thought over the story Mr Nap had told him. He thought it one of the best stories he had ever heard. The next day he looked for Mr Nap in the exercise yard, to tell him so. But Mr Nap was not there. The next day Hartree looked for him again. Still he did not appear. It was a week from the day when Hartree had first heard the name of the Lady Mary that he met the storyteller again. Mr Nap was running on the spot in a corner of the yard. Hartree went and ran beside him. I wanted to tell you, he said, how good I thought your story. I didn't finish it, said Mr Nap. You mean that there is more? said Hartree with excitement. There is more, said Mr Nap. And he began to tell the more of it, as follows: Lord Fox had been invited to dine with us on New Year's Day. My sister did not cancel the invitation because of what she now knew about him. So he came, and was his usual self, the heart of charm, the soul of wit. Ted and I were ready to fall in with his pleasantness, just as we had always been. But the Lady Mary was not. She sat stroking spoons until after dinner, when Lord Fox turned to her with an abrupt smile and said: You are quiet this evening, my dear. Lady Mary did not look at him, but she answered sidelong, it is because of a strange dream I had on Christmas Day. Dreams, said Lord Fox, always make me wake up feeling hungry. I do not think that you would like this one, said Lady Mary. But Lord Fox insisted that he would like it, and Ted and I said that we were curious to hear it too, so Lady Mary began telling it, and this is what she said: I dreamt that I visited your house, Lord Fox, just as you invited me to. I set out north of north, east of east, south of south, and west of west, and in no time at all I found it: Bold House. I knocked on the door, Lord Fox, but there was no answer, so I went in, and down the long dark hall, and up the turning stair, round and round, until I came to the gallery. That gallery I went down, Lord Fox, and at the end of it I found a door. And on the door some words were written. Lord Fox was frowning at my sister, sir, frowning, frowning, as though he would think her out of existence. Really? he said. Really, said Lady Mary. Oh, but in the dream, she added. Strange dream, said Lord Fox. Tell me, dear lady, he pursued, what did the words say? They said, said Lady Mary, be bold, be bold, but not too bold, lest that your heart's blood should run cold. But remember, she added, that this is only a dream, and of course it is not so in your real house, is it? It is not so, said Lord Fox readily. Nor was it so, he added. Precisely, said Lady Mary. Well, she went on, I opened the door of the room at the end of the gallery and went in, Lord Fox, and there I found, all in my dream, of course, skeletons on hooks, and tubs full of blood, and subtle skulls galore. And the floor, Lord Fox, the floor was strewn with coils of human hair. But of course, it is not so in your real house, is it? Lord Fox snapped his cigarette in half. It is not so, he muttered, nor it was not so. Precisely, said Lady Mary. Well, she went on, I did not stay to look long at that room. In my strange dream, that is, Lord Fox. But looking from the window, looking from the little diamond-shaped window, leaning to look across the sill of that little window with the leaded panes in shapes of hearts and diamonds, I saw you, Lord Fox, coming through the snow across the lawns, and you had your collar up, Lord Fox, and your drawn sword in your left hand, naked naked sword, naked naked hand, your naked sword in your naked hand, those nakednesses touching, and with your right hand, also naked, you dragged a poor shrieking girl by the hair. Good heavens, said Ted. What a nightmare, I added, why, Lord Fox, if any of this dark dream of my sister's were the least bit true, you would be a monster, sir, a devil in disguise. That's right, said Lady Mary, but it is not so, is it, Lord Fox? Lord Fox was sweating now. His eyes went to and fro. His hands shook. He pulled on his gloves. His fingers played with each other, touching through the skin of the gloves. They were yellow gloves, made of kidskin. My poor dead father had a dictionary bound in the same substance. Lord Fox opened his mouth. It is not so, he said, his voice like dead leaves. It is not so, he said, nor it was not so, and God forbid it should be so. My sister ignored him. I hid myself under the stair, she went on. You came in, Lord Fox, and you did not see me. You came in and you did not see me there. You dragged the poor girl down the hall. She was kicking and fighting and begging you, Lord Fox, begging you most piteously to let her go. But you had no pity, Lord Fox. You started to drag her up the stair. Enough, cried Lord Fox. It is not so, he cried. Nor was it so, he cried. And God forbid it should be so, he added. She caught hold of the banister to try to stop you, said Lady Mary, and you struck at her hand, which had a silver bracelet about the wrist, you struck at her hand, Lord Fox, and you cut her hand off, Lord Fox, you cut her hand off. Cut. Cut. No, no, no, cried Lord Fox, no, no, no, no, no. It is not so, nor it was not so, and God forbid it should be so! Be calm, Lord Fox, said Edward, moving his hand up and down his sword-hilt, be calm, be calm, sir, for my sister merely tells her dream. Her dream, said I, fingering my own good sword. No dream, said the Lady Mary. No dream at all, Lord Fox, she cried, for it is so, and it was so, and here the hand I have to show! And my sister snatched the hand and its silver bracelet from her lap, and threw them in Lord Fox's face. The devil roared with rage. He ran to the door. But we had locked it. Then he was at the window, clawing, but not before us. For we had known, known from the start, that our sister's dream was not a dream. We met him with our swords, Ted and I, and we fell upon him, and cut him into a hundred tiny pieces. And we threw the hundred pieces into the sea, where they boiled and hissed and turned the water black as pitch before they sank from sight and were never seen again. Mr Nap stopped. That, he said, is the end. A good story, said Hartree. I do not know, he added, which half I liked the better. Mr Nap looked at him, then he stopped looking at him, then he went away. Come back, mouthed Hartree, without speaking. Mr Nap did not come back. Nor did Hartree see him again during his time in that prison. On the day of his release he asked a screw what had happened to the distinguished fellow with the white hair who had exercised beside him in the yard. Had he gone home? Had he escaped? Had he been moved to another prison? Not at all, said the screw, that was Jack Nap the murderer. Murder? said Hartree. Didn't you hear of the case, said the screw, he cut up his sister with a carving knife. She'd been having it off with a Spaniard, he explained, just enjoying herself, poor girl, you know how it is, some brothers are that jealous. What happened to him though? Hartree demanded. He went for a long walk, said the screw. Hartree asked no more questions. He had been in prison long enough to know what that meant. The walk in question is done with a hank of rope about one's neck. It does not end in sights.

All the damage at the workhouse is to the back and front of the building, the sides being unharmed. Two chimney-stacks crashed through the roof, while others are twisted. One of the chimneys on the infirmary was hurled into the warden's garden. A mirror cracked, some books were spilled from a shelf, and six bricks fell down the chimney into the men's dormitory. Mr Duggan, the warden, is thirty-nine and looks forty. In 1891 he gave up talking, and since then has communicated by means of an alphabet board. He has microphones fitted to the brass undersides of the beds, transmitters pasted inside the paper covering the backs of the family portraits, and one-way mirrors in both the lavatories. At five o'clock every evening it is time for the feeding of his guinea pigs. The little creatures nibbling at the green leaves make him smile. Quink, leaning out of his bedroom window, drops an ejaculatory remark in the grass. Ha, he says, guinea pigs, guinea pig tea, ignorance is bliss. By the way, he adds, I've just noticed that Ezra vii, 21 employs every letter of the alphabet save j. Mr Duggan is indifferent to Quink. Without raising his eyes, he replies on his alphabet board. We are not always awake when we are not asleep, he observes. Ha, says Quink, mnemotechnics. Quink's first name is Jack. He was christened John but prefers Jack because John is such an unlucky name. Consider the early popes called John. The first died in prison. The fourth was accused of heresy. The eighth was a transvestite who poisoned himself. The twelfth was deposed for sacrilege and, as if that was not good enough, assassinated. The twenty-first was crushed to death when his palace fell down. Popes John who came between were all nonentities. And royal Johns, as Quink never tires of pointing out, have fared no better. John I of France reigned for only a week-end. John of Bohemia was killed at Cressy. John I of Constantinople was poisoned by Basil, his eunuch. John IV had his eyes put out. John of Suabia murdered his father. John II of Aragon spent his whole life at war with his own son. Impressed by this maybe, John Stuart changed his name to Robert when he got the throne of Scotland. All things considered, Quink thinks there is a good case for beginning a campaign to have John Bull changed to Jack by Act of Parliament.

At Barr's Court railway station all seven chimney-stacks are shattered, the one over the left-luggage office having fallen on the track. The goods office is undermined. The stationmaster's name is Pountney. Pountney considers himself to be the Assistant General Manager of the world. His voice sneers at its own wit, as if he regularly sharpened his tongue on his hollow teeth, or his intelligence on his self-mistrust, or something. He likes to work in an outfit like a monk's, but a luxurious monk – a white house-gown with a gold tasselled girdle. Thus equipped, with champagne fretting in the glass at his elbow, he masters the station. He loves white shoulders, the energy of his own imagination, outwitting his creditors, and kicking Johnson the porter. The year after he was born his father took off from London in a balloon. The balloon carried a cat and a dog, a pigeon in a cage, a bottle of wine, a cold chicken and a little picnic lunch, plus two wings in case of emergency and a pair of oars with which Pountney senior intended to row through the blue, all this in the presence of the Prince of Wales and a crowd of 150,000 who followed the prince's example by taking off their hats and standing in reverent silence as the aeronaut disappeared upwards. Pountney senior drank his wine over North London and only descended when his cat began to feel the cold. He taught his son the spartan vices. When a gentleman has had his arms and legs broken, he used to say, and two sword-thrusts through his body, then, and not till then, he may say, really, I don't feel well. Once when Pountney was eleven he fell and broke his arm when walking in the hills. His father told him not to tell his mother because she had been looking peakish and the news might put her off her food. Yet there was an occasional unexpected gentleness in Pountney's upbringing also – his father did not approve of children being wakened too abruptly, for instance, so he would wake his son by singing to him, softly at first, then getting louder and louder until he had called the boy back to the waking world. Yesterday, at four o'clock, after a hard day's work, our worthy stationmaster reached Seldom House. He is informed that Lady Glade is in the white drawing-room and has callers. Tea has been served. There are some half-a-dozen drinkers, men and women, inquirers after Lord Glade's wound. The morning papers have reported considerable improvement. Heads are turned as Pountney enters. Lady Glade rises. There is some disturbance between them, crossing it the stationmaster stumbles. His ugly face goes red. Lady Glade holds out her hand to him. The architecture of her smile is credible, but rococo. Pountney limps to glimpse it. She introduces the stationmaster to Mrs Justice Saba and a Dr Tool, a clergyman. She offers him tea. He takes a cup. He looks about him, not quite knowing where to sit. Come and talk to me, herr stationmaster, says La Saba. He might be a hobbledehoy schoolboy, back home for the hols, and she trying to put him at his ease. He seats himself, testicles itching, but the seat is narrower and lower than he has anticipated. There is a clatter as his teaspoon falls to the floor. One moment it is in the cup, the next on the floor, the longest moment the interval between, when it loops slowly through a silver arc of itself to the ground. Stooping to pick it up, Pountney slops tea over his trousers. His knees are wetted. He is angered with himself, angered that these people he despises, who are not worth a return ticket to Bangor, can inspire him with such a sense of awkwardness. Do tell me, Pountney, Saba commands, what they mean in the city when they talk of bears and bulls. Pountney's hobby is the stock exchange. This is a local joke, much giggled about in the Ladies Only compartments. A bull raises the price of stock, explains Pountney, and a bear depresses it. If he can, he adds gloomily. And you, mon cher stationmaster, are you a bull – or a bear? the female judge pursues.

Someone smiles. Pountney hears it. Madam, he says slowly, in his best sledge-hammer voice, I am neither a bull nor a bear – nor a cow. He falls to nursing his cup savagely. If they expect him to clear out, they are mistaken. As the door closes on the last of the visitors, Lady Glade waits. Pountney strides timidly across to her. In future, says she, the first to speak, if you must insult someone, insult me, you have purchased the right to. But not my guests, she adds. She tries to sweep past him. One of her blue curls flies loose. Pountney catches her by the wrist. He swings her round so that she faces him. Her skin is rough, his grip is rude. Don't talk to me like that Margot, he says. I won't have it I tell you. Do you hear me I will not have it. You are going out of your way to make trouble between us. Don't anger me Margot. Insult you what are you talking about? It's you who insult me go out of your way to do so. I don't want to be everlastingly hammering on the facts of the situation. I'm willing to forget them if you give me a chance Margot but you and your father use me my station to buy back the family reputation and your return for this is to treat me like dirt. Let me tell you this nothing is legally fixed up nothing. There will be no settlement of affairs till after our marriage. Now then we'll begin over again. You can reconsider your decision Margot. Only understand this I demand as my right that you treat me properly try to meet me. If you decide that things shall continue as they are I demand that the spirit as well as the letter of this engagement of ours shall be observed. I don't want emptiness Margot. I don't want cold looks and contempt. I have not done what I have done to win a shadow. I want the substance the real thing Margot. You've got it in your head that I want you as a stepping-stone. Can't I bring it home to you that I want you for yourself now that I love you. The vague emotions that at first he was unable to analyse have crystallized into a hooligan love. He releases her wrist. She sinks to the couch. She covers her face with her hands. The stationmaster drops on his wet knees before her. He sees as in a measure the pity and the tragedy of it all. However, he has no idea of giving her up. It does not enter his head. He tries to make amends by taking one of her cold wrists, and covering it with kisses. There, there, he cries hoarsely, there, there. And rising again to his feet he fans her desperately with his big hands, his country hands, his hands full of points and signals.

The total amount of damage to buildings in the city is, to the present writer's regret, not certainly known, but it must be considerable. Knox has collected a great deal of information on this subject from builders, with especial regard to damaged chimneys. In a letter received by your author on 9 February, he says: 140 chimneys have been repaired or are being repaired or are about to be repaired. I have no doubt now that more than 200 have suffered. Many of these were twisted. According to a mason, who has already mended 36 of the blighters, and has about a dozen more in hand, there is no rule to be discerned in the rotation of chimneystacks. They are twisted in every direction. Knox also mentions some curious instances of variations in earthquake intensity within a small area. In the glass, china, and earthenware establishment of Woolhope and Son, three shops away from King's building which has lost all its chimneys, only one vase fell from the glass shelf upon which it stood. Again, in Oatfield's similar establishment at the west end of High Street, three cups fell, whereas eighteen chimneys were shattered near the corner of Broad Street, and West Street, only about fifty yards distant. Knox adds a postscript which tells its own sad story. Mrs Justice Saba is crossing the road when she stops to let a car pass. When she tries to move, she finds that she cannot. Her flat wooden sandals are sticking to a patch of tar that is melting in the sun. La Saba tries to ease up her right foot. No go. She tries to ease up her left foot. Still no go. The more she struggles to pull her sandals free the deeper they sink into the soft, sticky tar. What a predicament. This is during a heatwave. She cannot slip out of her shoes and walk barefoot over the hot tar. That would burn her feet. Already she can feel the warmth of the tar through her shoes. To add to her distress, she is causing a traffic jam. Cars are piling up behind her. Coaches, a steam roller. Those at the back are expressing their opinions on their horns. By now the tar is beginning to seep over the sides of the sandals. Along comes the Reverend Doctor Tool on his bicycle if you don't mind. He brakes. He stops. He props his machine against the white wheel of a coach. He bows. Gallantly he lifts Mrs Justice Saba up out of her sandals. He carries her to the pavement. He sets her down barefoot on a patch of grassy shadow. Then he goes back to the middle of the road and tugs her sandals out of the tar.

Biographical Notes

Elizabeth Taylor

was born in Reading in 1912, went to the Abbey School, Reading until 1930 and then lived at her home near High Wycombe working as a governess. Later she worked as librarian, and in 1936 married John William Kendall Taylor. She has two children: a son and a daughter. Her first novel *At Mrs Lippincote's* was published in 1945. Since then she has written eleven more novels, the latest being *The Wedding Group*, published in 1968, and a book for children, *Mossy Trotter*. Her short stories are widely known and her last collection *A Dedicated Man and Other Stories* was much praised.

Dan Jacobson

was born in Johannesburg in 1929 and educated at Kimberley Boys' High School and Witwatersrand University. He has worked as a teacher, a journalist, in business and on an Israeli kibbutz, and has held appointments at American universities. He writes reviews and criticism and has published stories and articles in the *New Yorker*, *Commentary* and *Encounter*. In 1955 he won the Llewellyn Rhys Memorial Prize and in 1964 was joint winner of the Somerset Maugham award. His books include *A Long Way from London* (a collection of stories) and the novels *The Evidence of Love, The Trap, A Dance in the Sun, The Price of Diamonds, The Beginners,* and a new novel, based upon a story from the bible, *The Rape of Tamar,* which has just been published. He is married and lives in London with his wife and children.

Maggie Ross

was born and brought up in Essex. She went to Art School and then to the University of London, and taught Art before turning to writing as a career. Her short stories and plays have been broadcast and televised, and one of them – 'The Museum of Man' – formed the basis for her successful first novel *The Gasteropod* which won the James Tait Black Memorial Prize for the best novel of 1968. Her poems and criticism have been published internationally in many journals and magazines. She is married to playwright Barry Bermange and lives in London.

Robert Nye

was born in London in 1939. He is a full-time writer and has published three volumes of poems, *Juvenilia 1*, *Juvenilia 2*, and *Darker Ends*; a novel, *Doubtfire*; a book of short stories *Tales I Told My Mother*; several books for children, and a good deal of criticism in the form of review contributions to periodicals. He is married to Aileen Campbell, poet and painter. They live in Edinburgh with their six children. Philip Toynbee has written of his work: 'Macabre, Funny, eloquent and, above all, marvellously fresh in tone and manner. I believe Mr Nye is one of the very best of younger English writers.'

More about Penguins

Penguinews, which appears every month, contains details of all the new books issued by Penguins as they are published. From time to time it is supplemented by *Penguins in Print*, which is a complete list of all books published by Penguins which are in print. (There are well over three thousand of these.)

A specimen copy of *Penguinews* will be sent to you free on request, and you can become a subscriber for the price of the postage. For a year's issues (including the complete lists) please send 4s. if you live in the United Kingdom, or 8s. if you live elsewhere. Just write to Dept EP, Penguin Books Ltd, Harmondsworth, Middlesex, enclosing a cheque or postal order, and your name will be added to the mailing list.

Some other books published by Penguins are listed overleaf.

Note: *Penguinews* and *Penguins in Print* are not available in the U.S.A. or Canada

Other Fiction by the writers contained in this volume:

Elizabeth Taylor

*The Wedding Group**

Dan Jacobson

*The Beginners**
The Price of Diamonds†
The Trap and Dance in the Sun†

Maggie Ross

*The Gasteropod**

Penguin Modern Stories

The other volumes in this series

1* William Sansom Jean Rhys David Plante Bernard Malamud

2* John Updike Sylvia Plath Emanuel Litvinoff

3† Philip Roth Margaret Drabble Jay Neugeboren Giles Gordon

4† Sean O'Faolain Nadine Gordimer Shiva Naipal Isaac Babel

5† Penelope Gilliatt Benedict Krely Andrew Travers Anthony Burton

**Not for sale in the U.S.A.*
†*Not for sale in the U.S.A. or Canada*